Emil DeAndreis

Beyond Folly

Misadventures in
Substitute Teaching

Blue
Cubicle
Press

Beyond Folly
Misadventures in Substitute Teaching

Published by
Blue Cubicle Press, LLC
Post Office Box 250382
Plano, Texas 75025-0382

ISBN 978-1-938583-06-3
Library of Congress Control Number 2013901323

Printed in the United States of America

First Edition

Cover art adapted from C.W. Kahles's "The Little Red School Opens for the Season," with apologies.

To my parents,
for putting up with me.

Contents

The Ballad of Seamus

Annual Substitute Orientation

Horton Hagardy is sitting in his car, massaging his temples. He is downtown, parked near the hotel where this year's San Francisco Substitute Teachers Convention is being held. The clock in his car tells him there are three minutes before eight, three minutes before it begins. Other substitutes, his colleagues, cross the street toward the event with as much passion as bison loitering in a field. Horton looks down at the invitation, which states boldly that it also represents his *ticket in,* as though there is an eager audience that might exceed capacity.

> *We hope you are as excited as we are for the upcoming school year. This orientation will provide you helpful tools for the classroom! Look forward to seeing you! Breakfast* will *be provided.*

He got the notice a few weeks ago, a slip of mail that brought him more dread than jury duty, wedding registries, or notifications from the Department of Traffic, informing him that yes, the traffic light did catch him running that red light, and yes, it was going to cost that much.

Now it's one minute before eight.

Horton leaves his car and joins the other substitutes as they clump into the hotel. He gives a morning nod to a woman who he's seen at various substitute assignments. He is drawing a blank on her name, but remembers that she'll perform yoga poses mid-conversation. In classrooms, she is known to write on the board, while balancing one foot on her inner kneecap, creating a triangle with her legs. Horton was once in the faculty lounge as she engaged another staff member in a conversation while lying on her back, with her ankle pulled up around her ear. She is probably in her late thirties, relatively young for the profession. Today her yoga pants are a shiny off-yellow and her lipstick has been drawn past the perimeter of her lips.

Horton looks around at his colleagues and finds the scene eerily resembling an unemployment line. Together, they follow the signs that say "Orientation This Way!" into a windowless white room with circular tables and chairs. Horton quakes at the thought of the interactive work promised by this furniture. In the corner is the breakfast spread—bagels, Danishes, melon wedges, grapes, fruit juices, coffee thermoses, gleaming sausage pellets. In front of the room is a white board on which the day's agenda is written: words like *Welcome* and *Introductions* and *Formalities* and *Games*. Finally, in the middle of the board is the name of today's speaker:

Nader McCully, PhD Child Psychology Development in Secondary Education

Horton knows that name, a name from his past, a boy who went by Nads. This couldn't be him, though. There's no way the kid he knew ended up with a PhD in anything. But then again, how many people could there possibly be with the name Nader McCully?

* * *

They started as family friends, Horton and Nads; their mothers were members of the same Catholic church and therefore threw them together on the playground, in summer camps, and the church library during board meetings. They shared shovels when building sand castles and played Teenage Mutant Ninja Turtles on the schoolyard.

In school, kids made fun of Nads, not for his name, oddly enough, but for the constellations of freckles on his face.

"It's just how I was made. We're all different," Nads would sulk, a statement encouraged by adults as an alternative to violence and harsh language, a statement that adults don't realize morphs children into soft turds.

As they grew up, Nads started to find reasons to be offended by everything, not just freckle insults. Life became not about figuring things out, or handling issues on his own, but being offended whenever possible. At every opportunity, Nads tattled. Children were made to apologize to Nads for essentially committing no crime, and so naturally, Nads found he had few friends.

In fifth grade, the polarization between Nads and his classmates steepened with the beginning of Sex Ed, which, to elementary school students, was essentially a prolonged and multi-faceted joke. The image of pubic hairs, and the suggestion that they were normal, was seen as raunchy and worthy of celebration. The word fallopian was on a level of hilarity that fifth graders had never fathomed. One day, the fatigued Sex Ed teacher reached a point in her unit when she was to discuss the slang terms of reproductive organs. The schoolwide favorite turned out to be *gonads,* for understandable reasons. (Go)Nads McCully now had more fuel than ever on his trek to incriminate his peers; the rate at which he ran to teachers to tattle became incalculable.

* * *

The breakfast table at the orientation is drawing a range of reactions from the substitutes. Some fill their plates

3

methodically, with their eyes closed, as though sleepwalking in their kitchen. Others stack their bagels and Danishes like tires in a lot, considering it a small victory that the convention has provided enough food for seconds.

"I can barely even look at this food," one woman says. "I'm a vegan. Just the smell makes me sick."

She has a gourd-sized water bottle fastened to her waist that swings and clinks against things, inevitably drawing attention.

"What about the bagels?" Horton offers.

"Our bodies are not meant to digest processed wheat and flour."

"They're not? Since when?" asks a man in line, concerned.

"Do you ever wake up in the morning feeling stiff in your ankles, or tender in your ears or hair follicles?" she asks rather shortly.

"Tender in my hair?"

"That's your body telling you it's allergic to wheat."

"My *follicles*?" he asks, reaching for his bald head.

"What about that fruit over there?" Horton says, a pragmatist.

"*Cantaloupe*? I've been off of melon for ten years. It makes my Rheumatoid Arthritis flare up. You have any idea what that feels like?"

Horton takes his bagels and finds a seat next to an antique in a wheelchair, who is already asleep. Known as the Wheelchair Lady, and resembling Larry King with a perm, some shoulder pads and some pearls, she may be Earth's first substitute teacher. Her tried-and-true teaching method, as legend has it, is to wheel herself into a classroom, take attendance, wheel herself into the doorway as a blockade, and fall asleep. The running joke is that on the day when fish evolved legs, she was substitute teaching, asleep on shore, blocking the amphibians from taking their first steps on land.

A man with a grey suit and a sharp orange goatee has emerged from a side door. He is tall and fit with glassy blue eyes and a nametag that reads Nader. There's no doubt in Horton's mind now. It's more than the freckles that cover his face like busy ants on their hill. It's Nads.

"If you can hear me, clap once," he says quietly with a subtle grin, as though he is holding a secret. Some adults clap. Others haven't heard him over the sounds of mastication and light morning conversation.

"If you can hear me, clap twice," he says a little louder this time, pleased with himself. A few more adults join in. This is an exercise that Horton has seen teachers use to get the attention of kindergarteners. Consequently, he'd rather not clap.

"Thanks guys. That's a great exercise. An associate of mine came up with it. By herself. It can be found in her book *Teaching Without Words*. It really works. Thank you all for coming today," says Nader. "As the newest member of San Francisco's District Betterment Staff, I'd like to introduce myself. I'm Nader McCully, and I want to make it clear from the start that substitute teachers are *essential* to this district."

There is a grumbling hum of thanks.

"It takes bravery to step into an urban classroom as an unproven adult and expect results from the students."

"Yes!" says Bald Guy. He begins applauding, but aborts when no one joins.

"Let me tell you a little about myself and how I got involved in giving back to the community. For starters, growing up, popularity was not one of my strengths," Nader confesses. "Some might say I was an outcast, and truth be told, I don't have much of an argument in my defense. Over the years, I've been able to assess what estranged me, and time has also enabled me to *embrace* my past instead of wondering why things happened the way they did."

Horton is intrigued by the possibility of Nader, now a mature man, acknowledging that his childhood hardships were his own doing. Maybe now, as an adult with years of postgraduate exploits, he has wrapped his brain around the natural human tendency to renounce tattlers and instigators. Perhaps the acquisition of wisdom guaranteed by a PhD diploma has shaped him into a new person, a grounded person.

"One of the reasons I was left out, I've come to realize, is this."

Nader is now pointing to his freckles.

"These love spots. That's why. They were not a smash hit among my peers. Because I *looked* different, kids thought I *was* different, and so they treated me differently and didn't want to associate with me. Nice genes, huh? Thanks Mom and Dad!" He laughs, like a toy dog's sneeze.

"I remember having the feeling that I didn't belong, and that's why I got into this line of work. As teachers—be it substitutes or *regular* classroom teachers—it is our responsibility to create comfortable environments for our children."

Yoga Woman, who is sitting at Horton's table in what looks to be a painful pose, has just rolled her eyes.

"I don't like how he said that," she whispers. Others lean in to hear this. "He called full-time teachers regular."

The substitutes chew, mulling this over, awaiting her thesis. Wheelchair Lady sighs contemplatively, but in a deep sleep.

"He is inferring that we, the substitutes, are *irregular*."

"Ah," processes Bald Guy. The others continue to chew.

"We are not *estranged*."

Horton pretends to be jotting down notes so that he does not have to look at Yoga Woman and feel pressured to agree.

Nads goes on with his introductions, claiming that the most

basic element of child comfort is having his name known in a community. This is the topic on which Nader wrote his thesis, he says—children having their name known. Today, to reinforce that importance, Nader wants all of the adults in the room, about twenty-five in total, to go around and introduce themselves. This is to get familiar and perhaps feel the security that children do when people know their names.

"You know, we been coming to this thing for thirty years! Introducing ourselves in circles. We're adults! We're plenty *familiar* by now. Really, the only one we don't know is *you*," launches a mid-sixties man with a navy jumpsuit and a comb-over, a newspaper spread blatantly in front of him. To Horton, he's got the slouch of a retired gym teacher.

"Let's be honest, no one *cares* who knows our names by now!"

"We're too old for this!" Vegan decries.

When Horton started subbing, this orientation had young people who, like Horton, were a few years out of college and unsure of their careers. Twenty-five was a weird time in one's life. People moved back in with Mom and Dad, because in San Francisco, monthly rent rivals the cost of a new car. They returned to Gap and Starbucks—their college summer jobs—to work "just until they figured things out." Substitute teaching served as such a temporary job for some.

Occasionally, there are young, pretty girls at the orientation, and Horton is able to tune out the drudgery of the day and fantasize about them. Horton finds himself praying each year for their return, but typically, they don't last. For them, one year of subbing always turns out to be enough. They find real jobs, which deprives Horton of the periodic eye candy, and reminds him that he still hasn't figured things out.

Nads has herded the substitutes into a nice community circle to introduce themselves. The vegan woman looks unwell. When it is her turn to introduce herself, she defers. Nads asks her to please just *go along* with the activity. She says she will never just *go along* with anything: that's how women were denied suffrage. That's how the draft was instated, and white-only water fountains.

As the morning begins to sour, Nads develops a look on his face that Horton has seen before, a look of clenched and abrupt unease. His upper lip is slightly lifted, his mouth half open as if trying to say something.

"Yes, well if you would just tell us your name, we can move on with the activity. Please, just your name," Nads tremors.

"I haven't eaten anything today," she says. "I'm faint."

She is fanning herself. Befuddled, Nads looks at the buffet table.

"Oh sure," she bursts. "You'd like for me to eat that processed *cancer* to make it convenient for everyone. Just to *go along* with it, I suppose," she wheezes.

"Well, I—"

"You think I will compromise my politics for this rinky dink production?"

She braces the table for balance, having spent much energy on her harangue. People get up to bring her some food, any food. One substitute holds in front of her a Danish—she waves it away. Melon—she waves away. Bacon—she faints.

She is picked up and carried outside into fresh air by Jumpsuit Man. Nads chooses to stay inside, to hold down the fort. Clearly his PhD program did not prepare him for these spicy performances of human boldness.

Horton stares at Nads, who is still making the face, that contorted, irritating grimace, the origin of which Horton has just suddenly remembered.

* * *

In high school, San Francisco's Irish Center held an annual poetry competition, The Yeats Poetry Jump Off, at a school that was chosen at random. Everyone was welcome to enter as long as they attended the selected school.

The winner received five hundred dollars, not to mention a hell of a resume builder, and certain theories in life held that one's collegiate admission, and life path, was chiefly determined by his high school resume.

Horton's school was chosen his senior year, and given his Irish last name of Hagardy, he decided he might have a chance. With the last name of McCully, Nads also was feeling lucky and entered the competition.

That year the prompt was kept somewhat open ended:

Yeats wrote of many things like love, war, beauty, and life, as both an admirer and a cynic. Go out and wade through his catalog. Find something that strikes you. Find something with which you agree or disagree strongly enough to write a poem of your own. No restrictions of length or content, as that would contradict all our schools have taught you. May the luck of the Irish be with you!

Horton worked tirelessly on the contest. He read "An Irish Airman Foresees His Death" and "Sixteen Dead Men" and felt disgust for war and its disregard for life, but given that Horton was no soldier, had never lost a loved one to war, and had never seen the atrocities of war first hand, he didn't feel worthy of writing a war poem. He read "He Wishes for the Cloths of Heaven" and "Brown Penny" and felt a connection to Yeats's take on love as an unsolvable force that will plague even the wisest man eternally. Horton related because he was a virgin and could not for the life of him get rid of his virginity. Yet he chose not to write a love poem, because, once again, he feared his attempt would appear counterfeit in comparison to someone like Yeats. Finally, Horton found a poem on which he wanted to expand: "A Meditation in Time of War," a short poem which covered a topic much bigger than war. Horton spent days writing and editing his adaptation, exhibiting rare drive.

They announced the winners over the loudspeaker one morning in a school-wide address. Horton didn't hear his name because he was asleep, drooling into his sweatshirt in chemistry. Kids startled him so harshly with the news that he looked at them the way newborns look at strangers.

"Dude!" they laughed. "You won!"

Slowly, Horton registered what was happening. He rubbed his eyes and looked around, a bunch of kids looking at him, smiling as he processed the data.

"You won, Horton!"

The first person he registered *not* smiling was Nads, whose mouth was half open, his top lip drawn up as though he had just heard a tasteless joke. Horton had never seen this face on Nads. The look drew the class's attention away from the news at hand; people were more interested in Nads's defeat than anything else. They stared silently at Horton and Nads, essentially creating a showdown. That Nads had taken personal offense to his defeat was more riveting to the teens than Horton's victory. People quickly forgot that Horton had won anything.

Though they hadn't been friends in nearly a decade, this event cut all ties between Nads and Horton. They ceased to acknowledge each other in the hallways, though when they passed one another, sometimes Horton would catch Nads giving him that face. Horton hoped to never see something so ridiculous again, and he hadn't since high school, since Nads.

* * *

After Vegan was revived, she excused herself to a corner store to purchase a banana and some potato chips to level out her blood sugar. She didn't return.

Though he elected to abandon the Name Game, Nads carried forth with his sermon. Strategies for engaging children were introduced, strategies that had been researched and tested at the PhD level. They had names like Circle Map, Tree Map, Multi-Flow Map, Frayer Model, and Dot Chart. They all did the same thing, which was take two ideas and compare them.

Nads kept saying, "Now this strategy will be especially effective in grades five through seven." And, "Now this exercise *really* provokes meta-cognition in K through fifth graders."

This went on for hours.

At every opportunity, the subs verbally bludgeoned Nads.

"It's tough enough for us to get the kids to do *anything*! Who's going to fill out a *Multi-Flow Map*? What the hell are they anyway?"

"We're here learning about *charts!*" reinforced Jumpsuit Man from his newspaper.

"They really get kids thinking, *doing*," Nads ad-libbed, and then defended the fruits of his doctoral labors with words like *pedagogy*, *discourse*, *practicum*, and *praxis*.

"Oh *Jesus!*" a woman cried. "May I ask you how long you've spent in a classroom, Nader?"

Nads made a soft request to be addressed as Doctor Nader.

"How long?" she persisted.

"I underwent field studies for my thesis."

"The man's done *bubkis!*" Jumpsuit Man hollered without looking up from the sports section. "I been toying with this theory," he continued. "Hear me out, Doc. *I* think it's important that kids eat breakfast. Came up with it on my own."

Nads structured his mouth as though he had been presented a bouquet of farts. There were thirty minutes left, but Nads called it early, a rare moment of foresight.

The substitutes won. Nads was broken and psychologically trampled, off in the bathroom, regrouping as the substitutes gathered their things, picked at the scraps on the food table, and skedaddled. For the first time ever at a substitute convention, Horton found himself smiling. It was the best orientation yet—that is until Horton accidentally made eye contact with Nads as he returned from the bathroom.

* * *

Horton had a fondness for poetry after winning the prize. He wrote dozens of poems in the summer after he graduated, and upon beginning college, chose English as his major. He wasn't obsessed with poetry, per se, there just seemed to be no other fitting major. Business taught one to join a frat and to make "connections" through "networking," which to Horton was an intimidating concept. Philosophy and sociology taught students to speak freely of their recent feats of genius, and Horton was not one to have groundbreaking revelations. And the communications major: Horton found that no one could define *what* that even was. English was the only major that best spared him what he thought was discomfort. He chose poetry as his emphasis, intent to prove his high school award was no one-hit wonder.

When he graduated, he panicked. No job enabled him to exist as he had during college. He couldn't be a poet for a living. Even Poet Laureates had actual jobs. Horton briefly went into teaching, hoping that days with children might spare him the drudgery of adults in their nine-to-five jobs. He also knew he was unqualified and could never acquire the skills needed to enjoy, or even tolerate, the many nine-to-fives of the world.

So Horton found a nice job at a middle school as an English teacher while he took night classes for his credential. The kids were naïve and rebellious but Horton enjoyed them; their spunk kept him young, kept him in touch with the world, and he was fine with sacrificing his poetry time for kids. They inspired him; their imaginations trumped his. Their freewrites and nightly assignments yielded such creative and unknowingly poignant works; like self-loathing monologues through the eyes of a germ and stories of supermarket aisles revolting against supermarkets. One student argued that autumn was made of butterfly wings. Another wrote the story of a young boy who knew the meaning of life and hated it. They were brilliant in ways that astonished and fulfilled him, and sometimes made him envious.

If *teaching* were all that his job title inferred, Horton might still be teaching. But being an effective teacher and role model, he learned, was a very small and almost inconsequential detail on a long list of bullshit that dominated the life of a teacher.

Inevitably, correspondences with parents came into play. He got notes in his mailbox, messages on his answering machine, and personal emails about things from missing rainboots to requests for specific teaching adjustments; some things "weren't quite working for Skyler." Horton came to see that teachers were being expected to meet the extraordinary and individual needs of children while making sure they were all being treated equally. This movement was wholly supported by the principal and his administration, and so from every direction, the power was being milked away from Horton, the teacher.

He became short with his kids. There was a bitterness throbbing and compounding in him like a seizing back in Los

Angeles traffic, and poetry might have served as the acupunctural relief had he had any time. But between grading papers, lesson planning, replying to emails from parents, faculty, and department meetings (these twice-a-week, inescapable powwows that addressed and established nothing), Horton barely had time to have wine with dinner. If he did nothing about it, he would be a shrunken haggard worm by the time he was thirty, so he resigned and went into substitute teaching to concentrate on his poetry, and perhaps find a more practical career. This was what many would call a transition period.

A substitute teacher's job, as Horton learned, was to make sure kids did not get lost or die. That was it. It was a great job for someone in a transition period; only, he had been transitioning now for years.

* * *

"I thought you looked familiar," Nads says. He and Horton exchange soft rekindling handshakes. "I had no idea you were substitute teaching."

Horton nods, looking at the other substitutes—Jumpsuit Man, Yoga Lady, Bald Man—who are leaving. Wheelchair Lady is awake, wheeling away. Vegan's been gone for hours. Soon, Horton will be standing in the room alone, with Nads.

"So, how long have you been at it?" Nads asks. His energy, now that his day is done, is brutally positive, like a poodle unleashed at a dog park.

"This will be my fourth year subbing."

"No way. Wow. *Four years.*"

"They tend to blend over time."

"So what next then?" pushes Nads. "No way you could stand subbing forever. . . *could* you?"

Horton shrugs, feeling antsy as the room empties.

"So what'd you study in college?" asks Nads.

"Poetry."

"Ha! Unreal. I did Endo-Exo Communications, then got a PhD in Child Psychology Development in Secondary Education. So that's *Doctor* McCully to you now. Just kidding! How's subbing, the kids?"

"They're kids, in essence."

"What do you do all day? I heard subs don't do much. Seeing your colleagues today, I'm not surprised. They seem kinda *rough*. That fainting act, that man with the newspaper, that prune sleeping, the woman sitting like a pretzel all day, humming? Started wondering if there's a normal one! What do you *do*?"

"I try to write poetry."

"Ha! Poetry! No way. How'd *that* happen?"

"I guess after—"

"Don't tell me. After that prize? In *high school*? Ha! What a trip! We were so young. What was your poem about again? I remember I was so mad about that. That you won. I remember they told us in chemistry. I can't believe we took it seriously. It was just a contest. Remember how seriously you took it? Mine was about that one potato that grew underground without ever being picked, remember? Good thing I found a career. Was your poem even that good?"

"What is your job like, Nads, besides orientations?" Horton defers.

"What do I do? That's a tough question." Nads can't be happier to have been asked this. "Kind of difficult to explain. Well, I dialog, bounce ideas back and forth on advancement in education in San Francisco. Education is huge for kids, so I meet with district people, keep sort of an *open dialog*. We see if things work, approach them from different perspectives, establish model pedagogies that fit with the times and the individual needs of the students, continually modify the expected discourse in our system, introduce new philosophies."

"Pedagogies."

"Right, and with my PhD I get bumped up on the pay scale, meaning the least they can pay me a year now is eighty k. They *have* to. It feels good too, at the end of the day, knowing I'm getting paid that much to make a difference."

"My god."

"That's right. It truly is a blessing. Remember when we went to the same church?"

Horton looks at his watch and lies about catching the next bus.

"Nice catching up," Nads says as Horton throws his things together in haste. "I'm sure we'll run into each other from time to time. Though we are in different sectors, we are joined by a common yearning to educate!"

NEITHER OF US IS AN EDUCATOR, Horton wants to shout, but instead walks away.

"Good luck with the poems!" Nads calls, chuckling.

Horton joins the substitutes who have been moving so slowly that they are still there. They cough, grunt, and sneer. They limp, hack, and seize their ailing backs. Their awareness of their surroundings is dim and patchy. They are swallowed by the city streets and the buildings that tower above them, and everywhere Horton looks, he sees them. He is among them, walking slowly, barely keeping afloat, disappearing. He wants to think he is different from them, but he is a substitute teacher, and not much more. There is hardly anything distinguishing him from the rest. They leave him nowhere to go, much like his job.

He writes poems to distract himself from the fact that his job serves no purpose, yet he has still only written one poem that mattered, the first poem he ever wrote. He recites it to himself as he tries to separate from the insulation of his colleagues . . .

The Ballad of Seamus

There was one city block, which Seamus would walk,
A mist-riddled sliver of a much larger flock
Of esteemed ideas and updated beliefs,
And structured delusion and controlled disease.

The vapors of tyranny dissolving away,
'Twas a new day in Ireland, ye many did say.
They hollered and drank as they reveled the change
But Seamus just watched and found it a bit strange:

Dismembered soldiers returned to be limbed,
To ensure that no other would dare war again.
Racists were hanged, then the hangers in time,
To cleanse prejudice and slaughter of our minds.

Thought Seamus, what be there of change and resolve,
Aside from new words and earth further revolved.
What hope have we all if with this Irish rain,
We look into puddles and find things humane.

Beyond Folly

AP English

Horton Hagardy's father, Mickey, was a sheet metal worker whose job required him to wake up every morning in the dark and drive all around the Bay Area so that he was at the job site by seven. Some of these commutes took two hours easy. His lunch routine was to go to whichever taqueria was nearest the jobsite, down some greasy tacos, and promptly collapse in his work truck for the remainder of his break. As a kid, Horton worked with his dad in the summer, which meant he, too, had to wake up when the moon was still luminescent, drive to some suburb, flirt with heat stroke on metal roofs, and eat tacos. The only difference was that while Mickey sawed logs in the truck during lunch, Horton sat next to him, bitterly awake, for there was something about napping in a public parking lot at noon that made him uncomfortable. Mickey labeled this issue as "dainty," which was coincidentally the same label that he'd later assign to his son's decision to avoid blue-collar work altogether and study Romantic poetry in college.

As disappointed as Mickey was with his son's scholarly misjudgment, he was more devastated when Horton became a substitute teacher, because substitute teaching, he claimed, was not a career. It was a cop-out for those who were too lazy or mentally unstable to find real work. Mickey even likened it to unemployment and welfare.

When Horton had started subbing, he installed tinted windows in his car. Like his father, Horton had developed a dependence on lunchtime naps, which now took place in school parking lots, and not in front of taquerias, but he hadn't outgrown his issue with falling asleep in public. The steady flow of students, faculty, and parents made him jumpy, barring him from ever slipping into REM. The tinted windows protected him from the public, relaxed him, like the sleep equivalent of turning on a faucet to ease into taking a leak.

Now Horton had been subbing for a while. He was used to the routine of driving to different schools, handling new kids and new faculty and new rules, and then leaving, only to repeat the process each day. The tinted windows—Horton's self-installed cure to noontime insomnia—had begun to peel, but, thankfully, he no longer needed them. They were his training wheels, his water wings, and after three years, napping was now muscle memory for him. No longer did the taps of faculty shoes walking past or the shouts of nearing students startle him. No longer did he care if he was spotted as an unidentified male napping (and seemingly *living*) in his car in a sprawled or perhaps unprofessional position, because if he had learned anything as a substitute teacher, it was that weirder things have happened than a man napping in his car. Hell, they happened every day in San Francisco public schools alone.

It is an uncommonly bright morning in San Francisco, the kind where the sky's breadth is proved by the extraordinary depth of the clouds it holds, billowing vertically as if from a celestial chimney. Horton's view of this is thankfully tinted. He is in his car, parked one block from the high school he's been assigned, milking the minutes before the bell rings as if he was the student, not the teacher. The last twenty-four hours have been hectic for Horton and his family, leaving him with the kind of queasiness that is only made worse by bright mornings.

Last night, Horton's uncle, Hogan—Hogan Hagardy—suffered a heart attack. A sixty-two-year-old man, Hogan went public of his cardiac episode by changing his Facebook status to *having a heart attack, ambulance on the way*. Eight people proceeded to "like" this, though it was left unclear whether Hogan's friends "liked" the fact that the ambulance was on its way, or that he was having a heart attack. Minutes later, presumably while in the ambulance, Hogan "checked in" to the hospital with his cell phone.

Hogan's parents, who were ripe ninety-year-olds, learned of Hogan's recent lodgings from the early morning phone calls of strangers—Hogan's Facebook community—saying, "If there's anything we can do, Mr. and Mrs. Hagardy…"

"I'm sorry, who is this? *Face*book? Tell me again, *what's* happened to Hogan?" pled the parents.

When the Hagardy family learned Hogan would survive, they stopped caring about his recovery and obsessed over the fact that he had used Facebook to alert his distant high school alumnus and estranged Match.com acquaintances before notifying family.

"Is he suffering a midlife crisis?" one aunt worried.

"Does he secretly *hate* us?" Mickey asked, taking the saga personally. "Is this some passive aggressive *bull*?"

"What does it mean that people *liked* this?" sobbed the grandparents.

Up until that night, there was nothing more amusing to Horton than adults misusing technology and having their lives consequently blow up, like fifty-year-old men who get caught sending pictures of their wrinkly knobs to secretaries only to face headlining sexual harassment trials. Or high school football coaches who mean to send shots of their junk to mistresses—a modest greeting—but fail when lust swirls chaotically with glaucoma and arthritic thumbs and they end up posting the pornographic trinket to Facebook, which is then viewed by hundreds of minors. A cynic at heart, Horton has always found this to be the richest source of comedy, the raw salmon protein of laughter, but Uncle Hogan has tainted this for him. In his car before school, Horton cringes at the thought of his poor grandparents having to cope with their son's inconsideration in these changing times.

The bell will ring any minute. Horton drags toward the high school where he will teach Advanced Placement English. His assignment is something of a relief. There should be no disciplining issues, no headaches with these kids. In a perfect world, Horton would have a simple lesson plan which he could distribute, and, as the students worked quietly, he would send emails all day to his family members, reassuring them that Uncle Hogan's Facebook use was a momentary lapse of judgment linked to the delirium of a heart attack and a lack of oxygen to the brain.

Horton enters the classroom and discovers a poster of Malcolm X, the one in which the activist is sternly pointing his finger while saying a word beginning with "f" like "freedom," or "fight," or "future." Near the teacher's desk, stacked like sandbags at a military base, are boxes of assorted teas. The room is filled with foreign musical instruments, such as an egg-shaped flute with Chinese characters, a gourd with a net of beads fastened to it, and a didgeridoo, leading Horton to wonder if, and under what circumstances, the AP English curriculum calls for world music jamborees. He arrives at the lesson plan for the day, written in cursive on a Post-it in the center of the table.

Sub plans: facilitate a dense literary discussion.

Horton is not applauding these instructions. They will stifle his hopes of keeping his family at ease in this time of stress. Not to mention, a "literary" discussion that exhibits high levels of density . . . Horton wonders what that even is.

Students begin to enter. Each of them is nursing coffees in what seems to be an established routine. Scarves, French hats, bohemian capes, oddly framed spectacles, and outlandish totes are entering with them. Their lack of teenage energy is peculiar to Horton. Instead of texting frivolously with their phones, they are carrying books. Horton is also puzzled by their coffees, a drink he was used to seeing in the hands of adults in the throes of bitterly monotonous jobs.

"I have been instructed to facilitate a literary discussion with you, densely," says Horton, bypassing wordy deviations like "hello class" or "good morning" or "my name is Mr. Hagardy."

Students blink. Coffees are addressed.

"To what end?" queries a freckled and milky boy.

"To no end."

"Curious."

"Is there anything with regard to literature that you've been dying to get off of your chests?"

"What's your name?" asks another student in the back, this time a girl.

"Mr. Hagardy."

"Is that of Irish or Scottish descent?" she continues.

"Chinese," he says, wary of the girl's efforts to postpone the assignment. "Will that be all on my lineage?"

Silence confirms that Horton is the victor.

"So, how about that literature? What are you guys reading?"

"*Racing a Stopped Clock.*"

"I've never heard of it. By whom?" he asks.

"Joaquin Espacio Shoshanasburg."

Horton nods. "Is that a female or a male?"

"Both," a kid says. "Or neither. It shouldn't matter."

There is a pause.

"Well, what's it about?"

"It follows the paths of two young girls, a Jew fleeing extermination from a Latvian concentration camp and another girl as she follows the Yangtze River south to avoid rape and murder during the Nanking Massacre. As a result of their experiences, they are pacifists, naturally, but in the sixties, the worldwide movement for peace—more specifically war *protesting*—sweeps the two girls up and instills in them the very qualities they are trying to cleanse the world of. When they are grown women, sometime in the eighties, they cross paths. One kills the other."

"Refreshing," Horton sighs. "Who kills who?"

"It is never revealed. Because it doesn't matter," says a girl who seems to be purposely hosting a mustache.

"Right. So what is up with the title? Where do stopped clocks come in?"

"They don't. The title is an esoteric depiction of a world in which there are predestinies, things that are stuck how they are—i.e. stopped clocks—and in this case these predestinies, no matter our efforts—i.e. our *racing*—are violence, hatred."

"So no stopped clocks appear in the book?"

"Nope."

More or less, a literary dialog has been stimulated. One kid compares the title to another book he read once, *The Spinning World, Still*, a commentary on how our planet continues to age and overpopulate while its inhabitants do not progress or adjust—trapped, intent on repeating themselves for better or for worse. Horton asks if, at any point in *that* book, there are references to the title, such as a planet spinning, or not spinning, or if perhaps there are vague inferences to the solar system.

Nope.

Horton sits back and listens as the students proceed to ask each other, rather challengingly, who has read what books. Classics, contemporaries, and international masterpieces all come into play. Opinions on themes, social commentary, and the general fulfillment of these books are being aired. From one corner of the room a boy extols a book he recently read called *Suffocating from Air*. A girl says she read it, and that the ending of that book performed a thorough *gargalesis* on her yearning for neo-pragmatism. Another girl disagrees, stating that such an assessment is a bit exaggerated, and that *Suffocating from Air*, while masterful, only provided *knismesis* on her pursuit of neo-pragmatism in literature.

Horton can't keep up with this scholastic wizardry. With his degree, shouldn't *he* be the one stumping his students with literary terminology, separating himself from them with flabbergasting brains? He worries that his Romantic Poetry degree—when he thought it would make him a critical thinker, a deep questioner with flowery speech and impenetrable wit— has left him a faux intellect, inferior to high school kids. Perhaps his dad was right, and he should have been a sheet metal grunt all along.

"What in god's name is neo-pragmatism?" he asks.

"It's sort of self-explanatory," claims a boy in a Mr. Rogers-fashioned knit sweater and wooden clogs.

"Since *when?*"

The sequel to the acclaimed *Suffocating from Air*—*Starving off the Fat of the Land*—is due out later this year, apparently. Then the class moves on to another book that is praised as a classic: *The Pain of Numb*.

"The ending was so unexpected yet so tangibly subtle. But also *acute*," congratulates a student with a unibrow, a facial performance which would certainly offend Horton if he wasn't already offended by these book titles. It seems that as long as an author entitles his work with some vague contradiction, he or she is guaranteed a bestseller. He wonders when this trend started; only a handful of years ago he was in college, and none of this was happening, as far as he could tell.

Horton is frightened by how things change, how norms are remodeled and reassigned, how trends adjust and people adapt and embrace new realities. They're back to tight jeans and big hair. McDonalds is serving salads, cars are running on corn oil, sixty-year-old men are checking in on Facebook during heart attacks. No longer do book titles provide a handle on the book. The kids seem to know more than the adults. Horton is tempted to abolish this discussion and enforce a pop quiz on Romantic poetry, to refresh them of some literary roots and salvage any academic distance from them he can. He would ask who some of the Romantic era's distinguished poets were, and what the themes were of the period, beyond *love*. What about the repressive, revolutionary times could have helped shape these themes? What was William Blake really questioning in "The Tyger"? And most notably, what were the benefits of having such straightforward titles as "The Tyger"?

Horton waits for a lull in the class discussion, which has achieved a certain level of density, to administer this quiz. He waits, he even raises his hand to get their attention, but they never call on him. Quite sheepishly, he says, "Class? Excuse me, class?" but he is not acknowledged. Horton loses his steam.

The next book discussed is called *Waking Up, Dead*, followed by *A Flag Waving Without Wind*, which throttles Horton's psyche.

A rising intensity in the discussion shows the class has moved on to a new book, the title of which is unveiled too soon. Horton is not physically well enough to face the subject of the class's current fanfare, an opus entitled . . . *Breast Milk of a Man*.

Horton gasps, nearly suffocates . . . on air! He can take no more of this madness.

"Do I truly believe that this is the destination at which literature has arrived?" interrupts Horton. "*Breast Milk of a* Man?

"There was a time when a title had a role, a duty. It told you what you were getting into. Since when are titles erroneous cryptograms? *The Adventures of Huckleberry Finn? There's* a title, because you know what? With that title, you know there's a person named Huckleberry, and that he's about to have some adventures. *The Jungle Book*—a book. About the goddamned jungle! *The World According To Garp.* The title is *telling* you to expect some life perspectives from a guy called Garp! Are any of you familiar with the vital works of John Irving? Since when is it okay to stray from this and open the floodgates to this androgynous paradoxical clownery? It used to be that ideas were not pulled from thin air and sculpted flimsily into 'art.'" Horton uses his fingers as dramatic quotations to clinch this monologue, which is not met by his audience with any emotion.

"Little things that once implied a healthy functioning society are being flipped upside down and *everyone's* hopping on board! You can't count on anything. Everything is backwards! Grandpas are on Facebook, giggling and chatting like schoolgirls and posting pictures of themselves that no one needs to see, while you guys, kids, accelerate yourselves into the pseudo-cultured, cynical, and hypocritical lives of adults. Believe me, there's no rush!"

Quite gingerly, a boy raises his hand. Horton blinks abundantly. He is winded, flustered, working on an aneurism.

"Mr. Hagardy, there is a vein twitching out of your neck."

"Sounds like *knismesis*."

"Sure."

"Also," says a kid. "We read *Huck Finn* and *The Jungle Book*. In fourth grade."

"You'll have to forgive me," says Horton.

He is slumped, squinting with fatigue like a boxer after the twelfth round. "This is just one of the many misadventures of my morning."

He sighs.

"Against better judgment, I'll shed some light onto the aristocracy that is my extended family, and this may help explain my various short fuses today.

"Last night, my Uncle Hogan's heart blew up." Horton then details his uncle's proceedings with nausea.

"Can you imagine? A sixty-year-old in a stretcher, blood pressure gauges and oxygen masks and all, and he's dealing with Facebook."

Children are organically stunned, it appears.

"Judging by your expressions, I see you can relate to my pain."

"Mr. Hagardy, why are you upset with your uncle?"

"Huh?"

"All he did was ensure that the most people got the news through the quickest means."

"Oh no."

"He was probably in no condition to be speaking anyway. You *did* say he had an oxygen mask strapped to him. Who can make calls in that state? His methods were not impractical. On the contrary, they sound efficient and demonstrative of progressive thought, which is the whole point of Facebook. That's what it's all about. If anything, your Uncle Hogan has set the bar."

"I'm dizzy. My head is cascading into itself like molasses. Quick, someone throw me a cell phone. I must log on and shoot out a status of this cerebral lapse."

Horton dramatically collapses into his chair, with his hand on his forehead, amusing no one.

"This is *beyond* folly," scolds the unibrowed student.

"Beyond folly?"

Feeling cornered, Horton begins to hyperventilate.

"Why does this whole class speak like butlers from the Victorian age?"

"The phrase beyond folly appeared in a Kate Chopin short story we read earlier this semester. When a man's wife was behaving neurotically, he said that."

"Beyond folly? I'll tell you something that's *beyond folly*—all of you thinking Uncle Hogan is ahead of the curve! I'd have a right mind to alert the school district that none of you show the aptitude of Advanced Placement learners! That you are praising my uncle for his innovation suggests that our public school system as a whole has entered a state of crisis."

Horton pauses, once again breathless. He gasps as though he's been underwater, and suddenly he smiles. The patches that were blotching his vision dissipate into clarity. His smile widens.

"And in the same breath, I am oddly relieved."

Horton takes another cathartic inhale. The students sit, watching as their rent-a-teacher grins with renewed bipolar zest. Thankfully for them this is nothing they haven't been through before. This is just another one of those weird hiccups, glitches in their education, that is a substitute teacher.

"Unanimous support of Uncle Hogan could only come from the naivety of children," Horton decides. "You're not all grown up. You can regurgitate all the big words you've heard and read the books that cover adult topics until you feel like adults yourselves—but hallelujah, you are yet to grow up. Not *everything* has changed. Kids, by god, are still kids. Phew, for a minute there, I lost myself. You all had me fooled."

The bell rings. The boys stand and put their coats on and the girls brush their hair out of their eyes, walk over to the recycling, and politely dump their empty coffees. They carry on as though they've just watched a bizarre film and are now walking out of the theater and returning to reality.

Horton recalls one of the abominable book titles that had been addressed in the discussion earlier, *The Spinning World, Still*. The world's not spinning *still*, Horton thinks. It's not stuck. It's moving, *fast*. It's spinning a whole shit storm of ways—askew, drastically, top-heavily, unpredictably, torturously, irreparably—everywhere but still. *That's* the reality. What a crock of a book title *that* was.

Horton needs his nap, and it's only second period. He longs to mosey through the children and faculty and lock himself inside his cocoon. He finds himself thinking about his father, admiring him for his ability to ignore the bustle and chaos outside to get some shuteye. Perhaps his dad was on to something all along. He can hear Mickey now:

I'll tell you how I did it. I didn't read poetry and become a substitute teacher, that's how. I wasn't fluffy enough for tinted windows.

That's what he'd say.

Good old Pops, wary of difference, averse to change, embittered by all societal fault: in a way, the Hagardy apple has not fallen far from its dysfunctional tree. Mickey would have taken a taco crap in his dungarees had he heard those Advanced

Placement kids talking the way they did in English class, and those book titles would have parked him in a coffin. Things are changing and everyone must keep up, whether or not Horton, or Mickey, or anyone else wants to. A new class is entering, intimidating Horton with glances of crippling genius. Maybe he should look into sheet metal work.

Beyond folly, Horton thinks, picturing the student with the generous bushel of pipe cleaner for an eyebrow. More children are trickling in, the world spinning.

Beyond Folly, he thinks again. This time he snorts a laugh that is peppered with mental decay. Now there's a book title.

String Cheese

High School English Language Development

Horton's workplace is never permanent. There are no offices or bathroom keys or parking spots to his name. Some subs find the inconsistency stressful, but Horton has learned to enjoy his ever-changing, citywide commutes. Since every neighborhood in San Francisco has unique culinary histories and features, Horton has come to use substitute teaching to embrace the cuisine of San Francisco's diverse neighborhoods.

On days when he is in the Fillmore district, Horton eats sushi, given its proximity to Japantown. In the Tenderloin, he eats pho, as the district historically hosts Vietnamese immigrants. (It also historically hosts muscular transvestites and future murderers, but that particular demographic offers less in terms of cuisine.) Of course, the Mission is San Francisco's haven for Mexican food, and while its lower socioeconomic class occasionally yields classroom truants, Horton is always delighted to cope with delinquency in exchange for a burrito.

Horton's assignment today, Caesar Chavez High School, cusps Mission Street. Ordinarily, this would tickle Horton with lunchtime fantasies of salsa bars; dollar tacos, garnished with onion and cilantro, and marinated steak; and combination enchilada plates. The dizzying cornucopia of mariachi music and chef's rolling their r's should make Horton salivate; however, his recent taqueria ventures have not fared well. He simply has not managed to eat a burrito without spilling it all over his crotch. Last time he taught at Caesar Chavez, there was a major spill. So bad, in fact, that by the time the salsa and hot sauce stains had dried in his reproductive equator, Horton's Mexican students had taken to calling him "Señor Aborto," translating roughly to "Mister Miscarriage." Today, Horton can only hope that the students have done what is only natural to do with any substitute, and forgotten him.

Horton's lesson plan says that his classes today will be mostly English-learning freshmen. This makes him a tad anxious, as no age group is more insecure than freshmen, and no group copes with these insecurities more maniacally. The minnows of an adolescent abyss, freshmen tend to settle into their big new environment by shrieking, at all possible junctures to be heard.

The morning bell rings and students fill the room, dialoging in Spanish with the rapidity of soccer broadcasters. Horton is quickly reminded that any Spanish he learned in high school is now mummified, locked away in some unsalvageable tomb of his mind.

"Class, I've written your assignment on the board," Horton says.

"No espeeka eenglace," states a kid, right off the bat. Horton sighs; in his experiences, English-learners will utilize the language barrier to ignore the substitute's already weightless commands.

Horton does something that is ill advised.

"Su instructor... eh... se *escribió* el trabajo en el...eh...el..."

He gives up this repugnant dialect and points to the board.

"*Cual es la palabra por eso?*"

"*No comprendemos su lengua Señor ABORTO!*" bursts a child, inviting laughter and fleets of paper airplane deployments.

"Fuck," mourns Horton under his breath.

These students clearly remember Horton's last visit, his salsa mishap, and now they are in hysterics over his attempt at Spanish. He retires to his desk, gets out a pad of paper, and begins his process of writing a poem. Generally, words come to him for his first line, and from the first line, he then writes the last line. He ponders the direction of the poem. He got the idea from reading interviews with a favorite author, John Irving, who said he starts his novels with his last line. Unfortunately, today Horton can hardly put together a complete thought with the unrestrained Spanish chatter in the room. He drops his pen and looks at the students in horror as they ignore their classwork, shout with one another, and refer to Señor Aborto innumerably.

Horton has taken to whistling an invented melody as he dreams of lunch. He battles Mexican food fantasies, trying to think of foods that, if spilled, will not leave him looking like a blundered male abortion—things like bananas, salami, crackers, potato wedges *sans* ketchup.

Expertly folded paper airplanes are soaring, kids are laughing, music is spurting through phones, girls have plugged in hair straighteners and begun melting their hair into a desired shape, boys are practicing their incomprehensible graffiti tags on the board, which might later be inscribed on buses. Horton could fire off a musket and it might go unnoticed. For the next two periods, he sits, pen in hand, blank notepad, piercing headache.

"SIT DOWN!" snarls Horton as students enter for third period.

"*No hablo ingles*," says a boy quickly, almost involuntarily.

Girls laugh and address the boy, flirtatiously, as Esteban.

"*No se permite comida en la clase*," Horton grumbles in a nonexistent dialect. Esteban continues with his lunch. "Put your lunch away."

"No speeka eenglace."

Horton knows these students know *some* English. He has watched them process and comprehend him and then lie with their purposely mangled Spanglish. Horton cannot, however, *accuse* them of knowing English because somehow that would be exhibiting racism, or elitism, because of the small chance the kid didn't know English. That would make Horton just some grumpy detached goon who comes into schools and makes hasty assumptions about children, and it is not in San Francisco's curriculum to insinuate that newcomers must speak English or be chastised in front of their peers. It also is not in Horton's interest to exhibit elitism—he can't stand it, which is one of the reasons he went into teaching. Elitist students can be hard to come by in San Francisco public schools; the district harbors real kids, products of life, tough kids, funny kids, disadvantaged kids, honest kids, *good* kids. But goddamnit, these kids understand English, he *knows* it, and he can't stand their half-baked tactics to get out of work, or simply having to talk to the teacher.

"Class, your assignment is on the board!" he directs at his third period students.

"No speeka eenglace," says Esteban.

Horton sighs, thinks quietly.

"Let's see. *A ver* . . . What if I let you guys out to lunch a little early today?" he asks. He watches the class—which has clearly understood his proposal—mull it over. "Do you think the principal would be angry if I let you out say . . . twenty minutes early for lunch? A reward for your behavior?"

The students look at each other as if there is a briefcase next to them, stacked to the brim with hundred-dollar bills, with a sign next to it that says "*gratis.*"

"No," chirps one.

"No."

"No," chirps another, giving the class looks of reinforcement.

"No, sir, our teacher no get mad. You no get in *trahbull,* sir. Our teacher *always* let us out early, teacher."

"You fell for it!" cries Esteban. "Why are you all so *stupid,* man?"

Horton walks over to him for a good old fashioned student-substitute standoff.

"Why do you all pretend to not understand English?" Horton asks. "Every time I am around English learners, they do the same thing, as if they're the first to ever think of it. 'No speeka eenglace, no speeka eenglace.' What the hell is wrong with you? Don't you guys *want* to know English? Don't you guys understand the advantages of being bilingual today?"

"No espeeka a eenglace," brags Esteban, who is looking through his lunch. Horton looks at the kid's Zip Lock bag: apples with the skin peeled off.

"Mommy peeled your apples for you, Esteban? That usually stops happening after kindergarten," stabs Horton. Esteban says nothing.

"*A ver.* What else? Peanut butter and jelly?" he asks. "Did mommy take the crust off the bread for you too?"

Horton invites himself into the boy's cartoonishly decorated lunchbox, pulls out some more items.

"Good god, son! How old are you?" he attacks. "*String cheese?*"

"Pues, *tu* eres el hombre con las manchas en su cucaracha, Señor Aborto," replies the boy coldly. The class snickers.

"What?" demands Horton. "What did you say? Want to go to the *principal's* office?"

Sending a child to the principal is one of the only threats a substitute has, a threat that no student actually fears when coming from a sub. Typically, when a student is sent to the principal, the principal sends the child straight to the school counselor, at which point the student is asked to explain himself. Then the student tells the counselor that there was a sub and that the class was in disarray. The counselor always takes the student's word for it because, in almost all cases, substitutes are inadequate, and so, for the rest of the period, the student and the counselor play board games and joke about the futility of subs.

Horton shrivels back to his desk. When the lunch bell rings, kids explode from the room. Only one student isn't in a terrible rush to leave, a short boy who moves like a mouse. With little bursts of steps, as though sniffing the air to determine if it's safe, he approaches Horton's desk.

"I thought you should know, teacher, that Esteban, the boy who ate the lunch, he is in your later class. With some of the rest of us, sir."

Horton pinches the bridge of his nose. The boy shrugs worriedly.

"Will you tell me something else, young man?"

"Yes."

"What did Esteban say to me at the end of class?"

"Oh. Um. Teacher, he said you're the man with the stains on his . . . cockroach, sir."

"Divine."

"Because they call you Señor Aborto, because you had the stains, sir."

"Yes, that will be all."

"Have a good lunch, teacher."

Horton returns from the Mission Street market with dry snacks and takes them to the faculty lounge, where he will be guaranteed immunity from freshmen. When he enters, he is nearly leveled by the humidity of audacious curries. Joining forces with the curries are the exhalations of other dishes— lentils, kim chi piles, and gefilte fish. Horton's glasses fog as he goes through his grocery bag. First, he eats tortilla chips. Then, a banana. He enjoys reaching around in his bag like this. It reminds him of being a kid on Halloween when he would dig in a barrel of candy, excited by the possibilities. After a pear, Horton has exhausted the contents of his lunch. He is balling up the bag to throw away when he realizes there is something else in there, something thin and squishy, so small that he wonders if he is feeling anything at all. Horton reaches into the bag, takes his hand out, and is holding string cheese.

Horton does not remember buying it, yet his stomach growls, intrigued by childish dairy. So as not to be seen by the adults whose lunches were far more advanced than toy cheese, Horton is secretive with the snack. After all, how could a man who has freshly berated a child for eating string cheese then be seen with it himself?

String cheese tastes different than other cheeses, Horton decides as he chews. Perhaps it's the salt, or chewiness, but for whatever reason, it reminds him of childhood. With his eyes closed, Horton recalls the food bartering that would take place on the schoolyards of his youth—Oreos for chocolate milk, pretzels for goldfish, yogurt for dry Ramen noodles, trail mix for string cheese—and how kids left carrot sticks and orange slices for seagulls to battle over after lunch.

He peels the next piece thinner to make it last. Horton is now remembering football games on the blacktop and looking around to see if girls were watching. He recalls his crushes, playing footsie in class, and falling hopelessly in love after those brief, spleen-tingling moments when his hand would touch another girl's long enough for them both to know what was happening. The stick of cheese is getting smaller. Horton hasn't opened his eyes; he looks like a bad actor dramatizing the euphoria of hard drugs. He remembers kindergarten and how when he was but a young Horton, he cried, messy sobs and hiccups and all, when his mom dropped him off and said, "Horton, Mommy's got to go to work now." Sometimes it would make Horton's mom cry just watching her Horton come so miserably undone, day after day. The taste of string cheese reminds Horton of the salt of drying tears, of making lifelong friends, of learning times tables, of being an all-star kickball player, of Saturday cartoons, of holding hands with grownups when crossing the street, and most of all—of wanting more string cheese.

With the snack half gone, Horton's memories are cut short by a woman in the corner of the faculty lounge. She is slurping a Tupperware trough of noodles, breathing them into her mouth with a blank stare. Before swallowing, she is already bringing another fork load to her mouth. No daydream can survive this rowdy massacre of food. She is hunched over, pale, balding, flabby; she *is* the noodles. Horton watches in horror. She rises, and Horton thinks she will leave and that he might be able to return to his reverie, but she's going to the microwave. As her food reheats, she cleans her teeth with her tongue, making noises that are somehow louder and wetter than her feasting. She belches, *bwaaaaaaap*. The other teachers in the room continue to stare at walls and out windows, chewing obliviously like grazing cows. Horton must leave. He scoots his chair out and jumps toward the door to be liberated from this funky inferno.

In his rush, his cheese drops to the floor, and when he picks it up, he finds it has collected sand, crumbs, and eyelashes. Instead of discarding it, he holds the lint-pocked memento close to his person so that he can smuggle it inside the restroom and clean it privately. The thought of being seen with string cheese mortifies him. But even worse is the thought of string cheese going to waste.

He rushes toward the bathroom like someone who really has to go, cradling the cheese like a broken-necked hummingbird. Inside, he scrubs the cheese to his hygienic standard, at which point he peels it apart, thin ribbon by fragile, beautiful thin ribbon, eating it in front of the mirror. He sees that he is beginning to age. The areas under his eyes have darkened. He may even be witnessing the beginning of *wrinkles*, and his double chin, despite efforts to exercise, is decidedly content where it is.

The last of his string cheese is gone.

Lunch is over, and freshmen are their worst after lunch; nothing is harder for them than to quietly follow directions after an hour of freedom. Transition period is the term for the duration of time when students don't feel like shutting the fuck up. The presence of a substitute always hampers transition periods. Esteban arrives late with his lunchbox under his arm. Immediately, he is digging through his lunch.

"*Almuerzo ha terminado*," says Horton. Esteban offers no reaction. "The rest of you please begin working on your assignments."

Esteban takes this opportunity to pull out and eat his string cheese, stripping the plastic wrapping down like invisible bark of an albino log. He stares at Horton bravely throughout the defiant act. Students look at Horton, expecting a terrible reaction. He gives none. Instead, he is serene, unconcerned that Esteban is breaking rules. He is interested in Esteban's string cheese, wondering which methods he will apply to its consumption, as of course there are many methods. Will

Esteban peel off large portions at a time, or will he savor it and recognize that its taste can and should be prolonged?

Esteban rips off a dense, nearly unpliable column of the cheese and eats it horizontally like Bugs Bunny, grinding a carrot. Esteban is mocking Horton, eating not to enjoy the food but to rebel. Another sizeable piece is torn off, reducing the cheese to a flimsy rope. It kills Horton to see it happen this way. Esteban is swinging the cheese like a lasso. Horton wants to tell Esteban to take off smaller pieces, to take his time with the cheese and *enjoy* it, because once it's gone, Esteban will wish it back. Who doesn't want more string cheese, after all?

"NO FOOD in this classroom!" Horton blurts in a panic. "Put that food AWAY, Esteban."

But Horton is just a crusty sub, and historically, to high schoolers, no adult knows what the hell they're talking about, let alone a substitute. Esteban throws the last of it into his mouth.

Horton blinks, confused, watching Esteban's Adam's apple bulge and retract as the matter is swallowed. It's finished. Esteban crumbles the wrapper and smiles.

"*No hablo inglés*, Señor Aborto."

Some of his classmates gasp, others fidget, inventing work to do. The little mouse student is covering his eyes and peaking through the slits. Esteban sits, awaiting whatever punishment is in store.

Horton continues to stare, observing Esteban's angular shoulders and weak arms, his buds of acne and crooked teeth, which will probably be caged behind braces soon. He notes Esteban's pubescent voice, which neighs and screeches like a startled donkey. Not long ago, Esteban was in kindergarten, likely crying for his mother. Only a handful of years ago, he played tag and traded his lunch with his friends. Heck, he might *still* trick-or-treat.

Horton's eyes soften. He sighs and smiles about how moments ago he felt hatred toward the boy.

Horton's smirk seems to have put his students at unease, as though he is a treacherous clown offering them toys. He is giving the same smile—the same calm—that nature gives before an earthquake. Something is brewing. Something can't be right.

He walks over to the window and looks outside. Clouds like inflated rabbit's tails engulf the sun, casting large shadows across the ground.

"Say, let me ask you guys a question."

"No eenglace," Esteban reminds.

"Sure. Anyhow, would your teacher be upset if I let you out early?"

"You *tried* that already!" gripes Esteban in stellar English. "How stupid do you think we are?"

Horton walks over to the door, opens it, then stands right next to it.

"Well?"

"*Es una trampa. Está mintiendo,*" warns Esteban, looking at his classmates.

"I'm not lying. It's no trap. *Mira, hace calor afuera.* Go enjoy the sun, *niños.* While you can."

Esteban is, of course, skeptical, eyeing Horton with as much intimidation as his juvenility can produce.

"Fine," Esteban says. "I will leave." He calmly gathers his things, packs his lunch into his backpack, and gets up. At the door, he stops in front of Horton. They nod slowly at one another. Esteban takes one more step, gauging whether Horton will do something violent. He doesn't, and so Esteban bursts free before the manic substitute comes to his senses and changes his mind.

Horton stares at the rest of the class.

"Go on."

The students aren't sold, the fearful little freshmen. They look at one another for encouragement. Esteban is already outside, setting off car alarms.

"*Go!*" shouts Horton. "It's a beautiful day!"

Children start to pack their things. "That's it," says Horton. "That's it. Do something. Something fun. If you see the white rabbit, follow it wherever it goes."

Gradually, the class empties through the doorway, one student after another like young paratroopers who don't know where they'll land.

"*¿Cuál es el conejo blanco?*" one student whispers.

"Teacher," squeaks the little mouse boy, quaking at Horton's feet as though there is nothing more frightful than the chance to leave school early. "Are you sure we get to leave?"

"I'm sure."

"You said it's a nice day, teacher, but look, it's very cloudy."

Horton smiles at the boy, who is right. It's not a nice day, but that does not concern Horton. The students did not leave school today any smarter or better prepared for life; that does not concern him either. He has violated a fairly serious school policy by letting his students out early, into the streets. Horton is not concerned about this, either. Letting them be kids just one more day won't hurt anyone. Lord knows their childhoods will be gone before they are ready.

"Learn from Esteban," Horton tells the boy, just loud enough to be heard over the car alarms blowing up outside.

Baby Lambs
School Librarian

It is the buzzer-beater, beating rush-hour traffic, finding a wad
of cash on the ground. Ask any sub—that's how it feels to get
the librarian job. There is no better assignment because in a
library, the technology is too fragile and moody to be trusted in
the hands of a stranger. There are scanners, catalogs, barcodes,
and beeping things, which, if mishandled, can thwart a library's
homeostasis for good. Thus, in the event of an absent librarian,
lesson plans typically err on the side of caution, reading
something like:

> *Dear Substitute,*
>
> *I have cancelled all classroom visits to the library today. There
> will be no checking out of books. Please stay away from computer
> and catalog and scanner, as they are nearly impossible to replace.
> Have a wonderful day.*

Ergo, with no classes or tasks of any kind, the sub is almost
always promised the luxury of sitting in a heated, empty room
all day, with a lunch break.

Originally, Horton planned to take the day off; a late-night
stroll into the labyrinth of YouTube had kept him up late the
previous night, taking him everywhere from Rage Against the
Machine clips to tutorials on jellying cranberries. But when the
district called at five thirty that morning with the job of

librarian, how could he say no? It was the white whale of substitute jobs.

So, Horton rises from bed, splashes some water on his face, and puts on some old, comfortable khakis because he'll be doing a lot of sitting today. After breakfast and a jolly commute, he parks and skates across the street through the double-doors of the elementary school. The unmistakable scent of education is upon him—a cocktail of crayons, recycled poster paper, old heaters, and carpets. He walks into the office, signs into the binder for substitutes, and says good morning to the secretary.

"I'm a librarian!"

He gets his key for the day and heads into the library where he can taste the smell of old books with each breath. The hum of idle computers nearly soothes Horton into a nap already. A yellow piece of paper with large scribbles sits at the circulation desk. It reads *SUB PLANS*. Beneath that, there is one short line of instruction, Horton can tell. This is perfect.

Today there will be no classes coming to check out books.

"Niiiiiiiiiiiiiiiice," he revels.

But there's more.

Our school's Bring Your Parent to School Day is being held in the library today. Please set up the caucus table in the carpet area and assist Principal Rosepond, as needed. The library will be packed all day. Thanks, Mrs. Debbie.

"Caucus table?" worries Horton, as an image of Camelot's round table comes to mind—some colossal berg of lumber made for many men and their armor.

It all makes sense now, Horton thinks. Mrs. Debbie probably knew that the day would be tedious, and so she skedaddled the way many teachers skedaddle on days when bullshit is in store, like school rallies, parades, and department meetings. Horton thought he had lucked out, but it was a mirage. The library would not be an empty sanctuary of wall-to-wall carpeted tranquility.

He walks over to the burdensome oak that is the caucus table. It won't budge. There is a knock at the door. A parent has arrived.

"Hi," he announces, then finds a seat in a children's chair.

"Hi," returns Horton

"I'll be speaking today," he says. "I'm a parent."

"Nice."

"Name's Wald."

"Horton."

"I'm an environmental engineer."

The ensuing silence suggests that Wald would enjoy some praise for his job. Horton continues to be foiled by the table, getting low, as if pushing a Coup Deville through sand. Another few adults enter and gather on the colorful children's seats. They barter names and ask one another if they've come for *Bring Your Parent to School Day,* as though there could be any other reason for them to be in a school library.

"Boy, I sure need this," yawns a portly man about his McDonalds coffee—his McCafé. Crumbs and dandruff pollinate his polo shirt. He's gone on the record as being named Preston.

"I haven't been up this early since driver's ed," he says.

"You don't drive your child to school?" asks Wald.

"Oh, I don't have kids. My brother's kid goes here. He called me up last night and asked me to come do this thing and talk about what I do. I'm into sports. I'm a sports guy. Kids go nuts. You know how it goes."

A woman inaugurates herself into the discussion. Her elastic cotton skirt hugs against her hips, creating a half-wedgie that is oddly arousing. Her blouse hangs low, leaving little to the imagination regarding her bust.

"I'm Artemis, a dance teacher in the public schools. I believe teaching is nature's nectar of our future."

The men nod vaguely.

"Excuse me, are you the librarian?" she asks.

"I'm Horton. A substitute teacher," calls Horton, negotiating the caucus table.

"Substitutes get walked on by the students," Artemis informs the other adults. "They've got it worst. They have a *very* hard time earning respect, but they're the *real* heroes.

"Would you like some help with that table?" she asks, but by now the table is almost in place. Outside, muffled banter rises as students line up at the door. Teachers are peering in through cupped hands, gauging the readiness of the room.

Within minutes, the library carpet is suffocated under piles of young children, crawling on top of one another as they celebrate this postponement of school that is *Bring Your Parent to School Day*. Wald, Preston, Artemis, and others are sitting around the table, hands folded, as the principal silences her students with a clapping exercise: "If you can hear me clap once. If you can hear me clap twice, if you can hear me clap three times." The children follow instructions and the principal has their attention.

"Good morning boys and girls."

"Gooood mooorr-niiiiinng, Missss-essss Rooose-ponnnd," they say in unison.

Principal Rosepond thanks them for their salutation and then compliments specific children on things that they're doing correctly, like Jack, who is sitting up straight, and Tracy, who is sitting "criss-cross apple sauce," and Fergal whose big green eyes are looking right at hers. Principal Rosepond tells the students that they're in for a treat today.

"From the roads we walk on to the air we breathe, to the food we eat, to the power that lights our houses and turns on our computers and phones, to the trains, planes, and cars that get us to and fro—without people like your parents, things would be much different. So let's show these very important people how we treat our guests. Let's show them that *we* can be grown-ups, too. We can do this by listening, raising our hands when we have questions, and sitting with our heads up seven up. Right boys and girls?"

"YEAAAAAH!"

"And remember, as you listen to these special people talk about their jobs, imagine what our lives might be like if we *didn't* have them . . . "

Artemis stands abruptly.

"Good morning," she says, situating herself in front. "I'm Artemis. I'll go first. Journey and Eclipse are my children, sitting back there. I am a teacher of dance and spiritual betterment."

"Goooood Moooooornniiiiing, Arrrteeemmiiiisss!" say the children.

"Peace and love to you, gentle offspring. Boys and girls, from *La danca de los Machetes* of Mexico to the commemorative *Bon Odori* dance of Japan to the Palestinian wedding dance *Dabke*, dancing is nature's nectar of communication, of expression. My roots in the world extend deep."

Artemis leaves no doubt of her worldly ethos by pronouncing each dance in its native tongue; *La danza de los Machetes* is rolled out with rapid Mexican sass, *Bon Odori* is presented with a humble Eastern bow that nearly unloads one of her bosoms, and the "k" in the *Dabke* is hacked as though she is choking on owl pellets.

"How about this, boys and girls," she says. "I thought I would give you a quick dance lesson."

"YEAAAAAAAAAAAH!"

"How about the Palestinian wedding dance, *Dabke?*"

The children look at one another energetically. Horton finds them to be endearing.

"But first, let's pay the culture the respect—or *münasebet*—it deserves by pronouncing it correctly. Repeat after me. *Dab-kkkke.*"

"DAB- KEH," call the children.

"No no. Dab-kkkkkkke."

"DAB-KEH!" they return.

"No no. Let's not insult Palestine. We don't want to do that, do we?"

"Noooooooooooooooo," say the children, shaking their heads worriedly.

"Dab-kkkckkckkckkceh."

"DAB-KEH!"

Artemis sighs. "Someday, you'll understand. For now, let us all stand."

Artemis stands, somehow making it look like a religious moment. The students, all eighty of them, stand at once—a bad idea. Kids are high fiving, tripping on each other, pushing, falling, whining, chatting.

Mrs. Rosepond snaps her fingers, staring at Horton, motioning for him to get the children in order.

"Uh. Clap if you can hear me!" he attempts.

There is no change in their activity.

"Clap if you're *listening?*"

Now they're louder.

"One-two-three, eyes-on-me!" says Principal Rosepond.

"One, two! Eyes-on-you!" they say, and immediately shut up.

With their recovered attention, Artemis proceeds to instruct them to partner up.

"As partners, one will stand and look to the sky with his hands shaking like this, and the other will shake his hands, as well; look at the sky; and dance in circles around the standing partner, like this." She volunteers Horton to stand as she demonstrates the revolving dance.

"*KA HALA HALAHALA KA KCHCKCHCKEH!*"

Horton is suspicious that she is making this up. She gargles and leaps in what seems to be a conscious effort to be bludgeoned by her breasts. Then, she stops.

"Understand, boys and girls? Do you feel the spirit in the room?"

"YEEEEESSSSSSSSSSSS!" the children shout, chomping at the bit to show how cultured they can be.

"All right. On my count. And five, six, seven, eight!"

Artemis claps her wrists together, providing the beat with the clanking of her bracelets. Nothing can be heard, however, over the excitement of the kids. The vertigo of twirling drills children into the floor head first. One is already crying. A collision between two boys has inspired a tussle. Some students orbit into a bookshelf, knock it over, and spray books all over the floor. They are too excited to notice. *My Side of the Mountain, Number the Stars, A Series of Unfortunate Events*, and other masterpieces of children's literature shred to confetti beneath the sneakers of the munchkins. Artemis is aghast at the cultural inaccuracies of their dancing.

Meanwhile, from her chair, Principal Rosepond again has her gaze fixed on Horton, implying that his job is to solve this. The presence of a principal in the classroom has always ruffled Horton's feathers, for the principal is the closest thing Horton has to a boss. Usually, his job entails floating in and out of school without ever crossing paths with a single adult; hardly anyone ever checks up on subs, leaving Horton a hell of a margin for error. In the event of a principal, however, things quickly change. Suddenly, Horton is like any other worker, making unusual efforts to not displease his boss. So Horton fidgets to the front and tries to get the class's attention again.

"Um. Oh boy. One-two-three, this-should-stop!" he tries. "One-two-three, look-up-here!" he trumpets.

"One-two-three! Eyes on me!" Mrs. Rosepond says calmly.

"One, two! Eyes on you!" the children return. Their ruinous dance recital is extinguished. Artemis can hardly bring herself to smile. Mrs. Rosepond reminds the children to applaud and say thank you to Teacher Artemis for teaching them about the importance of dancing and culture.

"THAAAANK YOUU, TEEA-CHERRR AARRR-TEEEEM-ISSSSS," they squeal, certain that they are all now dancers.

Preston stands and says he'll go next. He sits at the front of the caucus table, his back molded in an arch that suggests a lifetime of video games.

"All right, let's get this party started. Let me ask you guys a question. WHO HERE LIKES SPORTS?"

The room goes apeshit.

"SPOOOOOORTS!" they yell.

Children who are too young to understand the concept of athletics and teams are looking around and joining in on the fanfare. Boys and girls who will grow to completely loathe all forms of competition are cheering now as though they can't go a day without ESPN.

"Me, too! Good morning, kids. My name is Preston. I don't have any kids. I'm Skyler's uncle. What's up buddy?" he says and waves at a kid.

"GOOOD MOOORNNIIIING, PRESSS-TTOOOONNN!!"

the children welcome.

"Whoa. Gotta love the energy. Boys and girls: I love all sports. My *passion* is football, though. Has been my whole life. I love the action, the competition, the teamwork, the brotherhood. I love it so much that when I grew up and had to get a real job, I figured, why not do sports?"

One oddball raises his hand and informs the room that his father plays for the Forty-Niners. Three more children say "Me, too!" Principal Rosepond smiles and whispers to the other adults that their fathers are actually all software engineers.

"Anyhow, since I loved football so much, I started my own fantasy football website, and now I compete with my own football teams!" Preston raves.

Children are quizzically nodding at one another.

"In my first season of fantasy football, I put together a nail-biting comeback and clawed to first place in my league! For someone's first year, that's unheard of! After that, I knew I had found my calling. Like everything else, fantasy football takes practice, hard work, and dedication, but it's been worth every minute!

"Hey! I bet you guys probably want to hear about my success, about what it takes to be me."

"YEAAAAAAAAAAAAAH!"

Bless their hearts, thinks Horton.

"I've got some general pointers for all fantasy football players, amateur and pro! One principle that has led to my consecutive championships is to never underestimate your opponent; as a rule of thumb, I assume that everyone in my league puts in as much work as me. This keeps me sharp, quick on my feet."

On your *computer* feet? Horton wonders.

"I make it a point to always be on my computer, clicking refresh on sports blogs, keeping up to date on injuries, trades, draft picks, stats, everything. I skip sleep, skip meals, anything to get that *edge*, and that's what makes me a cut above. You just gotta never give up! That's the life in professional fantasy. I'm living the dream!"

Professional fantasy. That's nice.

Having mistaken him for an *actual* football player in the *real* world, kids are grabbing pencil stubs and scraps of paper and scrambling up to Preston for autographs.

Preston is at the forefront of the twenty-first-century's American Dream, Horton decides as the children line up. He has found a niche in which he feels like a member of real society by existing in a fantasy. Working from home is the American Dream, creating a successful distraction—an *app*—is the American Dream. Working without having to work is the American Dream. In that sense, Horton has somewhat achieved Nirvana. Preston has it figured out, however. With the unjustifiable income, the pompous belly, the five-o'clock shadow, the unwashed hair, and the dandruffy shirt, he is truly living the American Dream.

When the line for autographs is exhausted, the children return to the rug, deliriously chatty from their signatures that read—in oafish cursive—Preston.

"What a treat," says Mrs. Rosepond. "Mr. Preston talked about some very important things, didn't he? Let me ask a question, boys and girls. Did Mr. Preston seem happy?"

"YEEESSSSSSSSSSSSSS!"

"Why was he happy?"

A child waves his hand. "Because he gets to be a football player! It's his favorite thing!"

"Right," she says, and then looks at Preston, his stomach, his posture. "A football player. But what did he say he had to *do* in order to become a football player?"

"He had to do lotsa hard work."

"That's right, students. So in order for Preston to be happy, he had to work hard first, right?"

"YEAAAAAAAHHHHH!"

Preston, from the looks of it, is deep in an American Dream of Artemis's boobs.

"Important life lessons. Let's say thank you to Preston for teaching us today."

"THAAAAAANK YOUU, PRREESSSS-TOONNNN!"

Charismatically impotent, Wald volunteers next. Horton prays this presentation be wholesome, inspiring, lasting—if not for the children, for him.

"Hey buds! I'm Wald! See that little goof over there, Ernest? Well, I'm his dad, and I'm an *environmental engineer*!"

Wald is horrified by the silence that follows.

"All right. Let me ask you guys a question. What are some things that we need to survive? What can't we *live* without?"

Hands are shooting up and flopping around like little salmon jumping upstream. One student declares medicine as vital, another claims hot dogs. Blankets receive some votes.

"Yes," agrees Wald. "Everyone loves these things, but try to think of things we can't *live* without."

"Food!" says one child.

"Air!"

"Ketchup!" fails one child.

"Water!"

"Bingo!" Wald celebrates. "Water! We can't live without it, can we? And if we waste it, or we run out of it, then we've got a problem don't we?"

"Yea, a *big* problem!" worries one kid.

"Well, every year, there are more and more people. So, as an environmental engineer, I'm part of a team that is always searching to find new ways to find clean drinking water."

"WHOOOOOOOOOA!"

Finally, Horton thinks. Something worthwhile.

"So, you know where we go for this new water source? I'll give you a hint. It's where Santa Claus lives!"

Wald has dropped the ace up his sleeve, the key to a child's heart.

"THE NOOOORTH POOOOOLE!"

"That's right. And is there lots of snow in the North Pole all the time?"

"YEAAAAAAHH!"

"And what is snow? It's just a bunch of really cold water, right? And in the North Pole, we melt it into water for everyone!"

"You take Santa's water?" asks a girl.

"Oh, we would never . . ."

"You burn down Santa's house?" frets a boy.

"Of course not . . ."

"Do you see Santa?"

"Well, no . . ."

"What about the elves?"

Wald is ruined, clearing his throat to bring the attention of the room back to his heroics, but he's lost them. They are talking about Santa, his favorite cookies, their gifts from last year, and their wish lists for this year. Kids are claiming they've seen Santa come down through their chimney, though most houses in San Francisco do not possess chimneys.

"Say, kids. You know what Santa's favorite drink is? Water!"

The children chatter, triggering the end of Wald. Horton is sitting in a baby chair, trying to wrap his mind around the concept of melting ice caps for water and calling it environmental engineering.

Artemis and Preston are discussing water; she has just claimed that it is the nectar of Earth's nipple, while Preston says he can "take it or leave it."

"A diet Mountain Dew and I'm good to go."

Suddenly, Horton is having trouble seeing the difference between the children and the adults. If he had a choice, though, he'd prefer the company of kids. Hell, he'd rather be on the rug talking about Santa Claus than up there with the adults. Horton thinks fondly of childhood, when having an imagination was a sign of a healthy promising mind, as opposed to then, when fantasizing turned you into Preston: a celibate, oval-shaped earthworm.

There is one person who hasn't yet presented. He hasn't spoken a word to anyone; he's barely even moved. No one knows his name or what he does or which child is his. There is a forgettable, mundane quality about him, a paleness in his face. He maneuvers himself to the front of the room and is standing before anyone notices.

"Salutations, young learners," he says. The children don't have any idea as to how to respond. "I look around this room and find your innocence enlivening. In your little eyes I see the wonder and the trust of baby lambs."

Horton looks at Principal Rosepond, wondering if she shares his concern that a pedophile is present.

"Please trust when I say that my sole purpose is to keep you out of harm's way. Sometimes the world is scary, and I mean to make it safe.

"For my job, I track down the bad people. I keep close watch of them, follow them. Recently, I've been a part of something groundbreaking. We've placed sound receptors in jails, prisons, juvenile detention centers, mental asylums, hospitals, and courtrooms. There, vocal samples of anyone who passes through are being recorded and stored in our database."

The confusion of the children and adults does not unsettle him, in fact, it provides a nice platform on which to proceed uninterrupted.

"With this information, we have created a phone application that can recognize the voices of criminals. Soon, we will all be able to hold our phones up to conversations and—within seconds—know if a criminal is nearby. How delightful. On the buses, in supermarkets, anywhere in the *world*, criminals will have no place to hide. Anyone who has ever spent a night in jail, anyone who has ever pled innocent to a speeding ticket, will be cataloged—forever.

"And once we've got this up and running, we'll begin constructing our Watch List, which will contain people who have not yet committed crimes, but show a proclivity for misdeeds. We will conspire closely with social networks like Facebook, and YouTube, combing through illicit material to determine who might be a future criminal. This Watch List, in time, will be accessible to all civilians, granting us the privacy that Americans deserve.

"Soon this application will be a treasured function of our everyday lives," he predicts. "We will wonder how we ever lived without it. We will forget that we ever *did* live without it."

The man gives no indication he is finished, yet he fades back to the caucus table.

Principal Rosepond forgets to tell the children to applaud. A silence takes over the room. Horton wishes he was a kid on the rug being mesmerized by these presenters. He wishes he thought they were role models, heroes, like they're supposed to be. He then worries if he has ever searched through anything on YouTube, or written anything in any correspondence that might land him on the CIA's Watch List. Horton feels the kind of queasiness one might have on a curvy, narrow, one-way road.

"My brother has Facebook!" says a child, breaking the silence.

"Yeaaaah!"

"Me, too!"

With no presenters left, the students explode into chats about Facebook, as they clearly do not understand what they just heard.

"Do you have Facebook?" Preston seriously asks Artemis. Horton thinks about what Mrs. Rosepond said prior to the event:

"And remember, as you listen to these special people talk about their jobs, imagine what our lives might be like if we didn't have them..."

Preston and Artemis have planned to be Facebook friends. Wald is busy offering samples of his water and the adults are *slurping* it up. The speaker from an unknown organization has continued his creepy streak by vanishing entirely.

"All right, all right, my baby lambs," cooes Principal Rosepond. "What a strange man that last man was, sweet and strange. Wasn't that a sweet thing he called the children? Baby lambs," she notes to the adults, who nod. "If you can hear me clap once," she calls, and the students respond.

Baby lambs, thinks Horton. What an apt label, for everyone.

Tray Bien!

Computer Lab Specialist

Horton wakes up one Monday to this assignment:

Assn #349832 COMPUTER LAB TECHNICIAN, MONROE MIDDLE SCHOOL

As unclear as Horton is on the specifics of this job, or how it even came to exist in public schools, he is fairly sure he'll have to do none of it today; he is no technician. He can update, collate, encode, and repair nothing. For these reasons, he finds himself looking forward to a stress-free workday. Yet, one thing nags him in the back of his mind.

Horton had been at Monroe Middle School a few months earlier. That was the school with Principal Tray, or Mr. *Tray Bien*—his self-issued nickname. Horton never wanted to sub there again. Rarely did he have bad experiences with faculty, for they typically kept to themselves; Principal Tray Bien, however, had a different agenda, one which was quite predatory toward Horton. As Horton dresses for the day, he recalls his previous experience at Monroe Middle School.

School got out at 2:40 p.m. Horton had just signed out and was leaving the office to go home, when he heard:

"Mr. Substitute? Yes, Mr. Substitute?"

Principal Tray was extending his hand. They shook, though they had met that morning and shaken hands then.

"Were you on your way out?"

"I was," said Horton.

"Yes, well, if you look carefully at the assignment details, technically your work day goes until four."

Mr. Tray looked at his watch even though he knew that it was exactly 2:45.

"So another hour and half or so? Is that going to work for you?"

Mr. Tray did not wait for an answer; he assumed it was going to work.

"You see," he went on, "our employees are required to stick around, you know, and put in a *normal* work day, like anyone else. The day doesn't end when the bell rings. *Real* teachers must grade papers and enter grades, talk to parents, prepare lesson plans. Janitors must clean. Paraprofessionals must assist in getting children on their proper buses. You see, these are simply the necessary nuts and bolts of a well-oiled choo choo."

The analogy of a well-oiled choo choo wasn't quite working for Horton. Neither was Principal Tray's glossy bald head and haystack mustache combo. Horton had a theory that bald people with mustaches were compensating for their loss, proving they could still somehow grow hair. Bald people with clean shaves had accepted their loss and moved on, while the mustache-wearing chrome domes had those furry little flags beneath their noses, waving as a reminder that they were still men.

"Oftentimes a substitute will be sent home when the school day ends, with a full day's pay, when in reality, he has not technically worked a full day. In my opinion, it's not much different than stealing. Do you follow?"

Of course Horton followed; he reaped the benefits of this flaw every day.

"As head of this institution, I don't feel it sets a good example, so if you don't mind, I'll just go ahead and find something for you to do. Is that all right with you?"

In general, Horton disliked being told he had to do something, disliked more when people took pleasure in explaining *why* he had to do it, and could not stand to be asked 'is that all right with you?' or 'will that work for you?' when in reality, it didn't matter whether or not it was going to work for anyone.

Principal Tray radioed the custodians to see if they might be able to invent some work for Horton, but their English was so defective and the walkie-talkies so full of static that Principal Tray had to search elsewhere. Finally, he placed Horton outside in the after-school program, which was on a field trip. So Horton stood outside, in a completely empty schoolyard, for one and a half hours.

Despite this cheerless memory, Horton decides to not cancel his job that day, reminding himself that everyone else has bosses they hate, and that he should be no exception. So, he grabs some food from the kitchen and drives to Monroe Middle School.

With stealthy efforts to avoid Mr. Tray in the office, Horton signs in and heads to his room of the day, the computer lab.

Students know their assignments. Leave attendance strips on my desk, thanks.

Horton grunts triumphantly.

The bell rings for homeroom. Horton pulls a poetry book from his bag, opens it to Lewis Carroll's poem "Jabberwocky."

> *'Twas brillig, and the slithy toves*
> *Did gyre and gimble in the wabe;*
> *All mimsy were the borogoves,*
> *And the mome raths outgrabe.*

Horton is asleep. He wakes up two hours later, without having had a single student enter.

Now there is commotion in the hallways. It is 11 a.m., third period. The door to the computer lab opens, letting in the wretched yodels of young teenagers. Two students enter and look at Horton.

"OH, WE GOT A FUCKING SUB!"

"YES!"

These two turds take themselves back into the hallway, where they continue to rejoice and alert the school. By the time the celebrations are wrapped up, class has technically been in session for ten minutes.

An elfish woman scoots into the room behind the students. She notes Horton and is promptly next to him.

"Shhhhhh. Classssss," she says. "Hi, I'm Randi. We've got the computer lab third period, it says so right here on the schedule. Third period, computer lab."

"Welcome," says Horton.

"I'm a substitute, so I'll need your help. *HISSSSSSS*."

"I'm also a sub," Horton replies. "I can only promise to do my best."

"I'm going to need your help."

Horton is fixated on the woman's nose. It seems intrusive, presumptuous. It's more of a beak, a long and curved scythe, a Tim Burton creation.

"Class, *sssssssssssshhhhhhh*. I'm going to turn you over to the computer lab specialist. He will give you your assignment. *HSSSSSSSSSSSSSSSS!* Please."

"Actually, I'm no specialist," says Horton. "I'm a sub. Your teacher says you know your assignments."

"We do," a student says.

"Are there any questions about the assignment?" Horton asks.

"No. We all know what to do," says another student.

Randi rises, does more slithering. "Quiet please. Quiet everyone. *Sssssssssssssshhhhhhhhhhhhhhhhhhhhhhhhhh.* Can you support me, please? I am going to need your help with this class," she directs at Horton. "I'm a sub."

Randi reminds Horton why he never fraternizes with other subs—*colleagues.* Their eccentricities are innumerable and potent. They have strong opinions on things no one has ever been compelled to think about. There is always something that's been bothering them. Some aren't prone to changing their clothes, others have a cycle of clothes that should not be worn in public. If allotted the opportunity, subs will jump into their life stories with emphasis on the dreary parts. Occasionally, Horton will suggest he is not listening by pulling out his phone, or waving at strangers, or walking away mid-story, only to be followed and forced to hear the rest. He has endured tales of marital fallouts, arrest records of nephews, and persistent rashes, from total strangers. They are overeager to reveal their harsh daily bouts with things like rheumatoid arthritis, claustrophobia, or explosive bunions, which prevent them from getting real jobs in the real world. Most find reasons to complain about subbing the way normal people complain about *real* jobs. Subbing is not a real job, and there is no clearer proof than the lunacy of its workforce. Horton wishes it wasn't true, but now, in his third year of subbing, he fears it can't be denied. He fears someday he will be just like them.

"They sure don't pay us enough for this, do they?" Randi gripes.

"For *what?*"

"Sssssssssssss."

Horton walks away. Randi follows.

"Sssssssssssssssss. I've found that this noise I make really helps quiet a class. Even if they're *already* quiet."

Horton nods, acknowledging Randi's trick of the trade.

"Sssssssssssssshhhhh. Everyone working. Sssssssssshhhhh. Working. Sssssssshhhhhh. Working quietly. Ssssssssssssssss. Please. Sssssssssss. Help."

The classroom phone rings.

"Where are you going?" panics Randi. "Hsssssssssssssssssss. Please, everyone. Sssssssshhhhhhhh. Calm."

Horton reaches for the phone.

"Hello? Computer lab."

"Hello, yes. With whom am I speaking?"

"This is Mr. Hagardy. A sub."

"Do you have a minute, Mr. Hagardy? You are speaking with Mr. Tray."

Horton would rather be hearing from the IRS.

"Good day."

"Mr. Hagardy, an issue has arisen, something that has left me a bit disappointed. You see, as overseer of this school, I feel it is my duty to know the schedule of everyone working under me. By knowing who is on break, who is on lunch, whose day starts late, and whose day ends early, I am in a much better position to be an effective leader. Yes?"

"Yes."

"Well, because I know my employees, I know that our regular computer lab teacher has no homeroom, and no classes for the first two periods of school. That's about two hours of zilch! What a lucky guy, what an easy morning. He usually spends that time updating the software on the computers and what not. He gets to school on time, every day, even though he doesn't start until eleven. That's how I prefer my workers."

"Okay."

"I like to check in on our visitors, Mr. Hagardy, to make sure everything is all right. You are a visitor. So when I came by your room

this morning to check up, you were napping. It was nine thirty, and you were out, for two periods, in a chair.

"If I recall correctly, we had similar issues with you cutting corners last time you were here. I am sure you remember trying to leave early, and how that worked out for you. I hope you don't think it is fair for you to get paid to catch up on some z's?"

"In the future, what would you like me to do?"

"Yes, hmmmm. Well, our secretary is swamped, Mr. Hagardy. Her job is actually very difficult. An extra hand in the office is always appreciated. That's a place where you can assume there is work to be done. In fact, next period is lunch. Have you made plans?"

Horton has a pear, a donut, and string cheese—a childhood snack which he has found himself eating unstoppably as of late. He has no plans, however, for lunch.

"No."

"Well then, if it's all right with you, Mr. Hagardy, I'm going to have you come down to the office during lunch and help out. You just come down and maybe we can keep you busy with something. Is that going to work for you?"

Of course it's going to work. What choice does Horton have? He hangs up and walks back to the lab, deciding again to never return to Monroe Middle School. That will show them. Someday, he will wake up to a phone call. "Good morning, Horton, this is Monroe Middle School, are you available this morning? We are desperate for a sub," they will say, and Horton will say, "I *am* available, thanks for asking! I will, however, not be coming to Monroe because your principal is a disassociated, self-important pile of shit!"

That will show them.

Randi is in the middle of what looks to be examining her hair to see if it is falling out. She walks up to Horton.

"I've got all these bills because my son goes to a private

university. I told him 'go to a junior college.' But they don't listen! Forty-five thousand a year in tuition! *SSSSSSSSSSSSSSSS*. If you think my ex-husband is helping out with the bills*sssssss*. You're wrong. I've got this weird lump on my ankle. I've paid over a hundred dollars on appointment*sssssssssssssssss*. *Ssssssssssssss*. Just to hear the doctors say they've never seen anything like it. If doctors can't diagnose or treat, *HSSSSSSS*, then I think they should have to give our money back. I am not paying an expert to tell me what he *doessssn't* know."

"I'm going to the bathroom," says Horton.

"My divorce is costing me an arm and a leg," Randi unravels. "I'd appreciate your assistance!"

Horton sits on the can with his pants on until there are five minutes left in the period. Then he goes to the water fountain and takes his time sipping. When he reenters the computer lab, the students are packing up their bags for lunch. The lunch bell rings. Randi says "adieu" and plunges into the malicious middle school hallway, likely to be trampled.

Horton grabs his bag and prepares for Principal *Tray Bien*. The hallways are filled with venomous monsters bouncing off metal lockers.

Horton pushes children as he advances toward Mr. Tray's lair. When he enters, Principal Tray is very *un*busy.

"Mr. Hagardy. Hello."

"Hello."

"Enter, please."

Horton has already entered. "Thank you," he lies.

"As said earlier, I've got some work for you to take care of. This way, we'll all feel better about your effort today. It will feel refreshing later tonight to know you earned your pay."

"Thanks."

"Do you think you can make some simple calls on behalf of

Monroe Middle School?"

"Phone calls?"

"Yes. Nothing terribly challenging, don't worry."

"Phone calls to whom?"

"Well, you see, Mr. Hagardy, it is a principal's dream to have his school run smoothly. I like to think of it as a well-oiled choo choo.

"There are nuts, bolts, conductors, coals . . . windows, uh, among other things that must be functioning for the train to work properly. Well, every once in a while, situations will come along and throw that choo choo out of whack. As you can imagine, I've handled them all. Following some recent events, Monroe Middle School has decided to let some students go."

"I see."

"You'll notice I've left the contact information, along with full names of the children and their parents that you'll be calling on my desk. I assume you will address them as mister or misses. Feel free to use my personal office phone. I've got to run for a lunch appointment."

"I'm expelling children?"

"We're letting some go. To begin a new life path."

"And you're leaving now?"

"That's right."

"What did these students do to get expelled?" asks Horton.

Mr. Tray twists his face in disappointment.

"Mr. Hagardy, at Monroe Middle School, the students come first; no matter their behavioral or socioeconomic issues, their privacy must be honored. Frankly, their expulsion is none of your business."

"Oh."

Mr. Tray leaves. Horton reviews his list of people to call. Some of the names are unbelievable. Horton takes a deep breath and dials. Four rings pass, at which point Horton is welcomed to this voicemail greeting:

*You got Crepe, if you're calling about the free puppies, sorry—we're keeping all of them. *BEEP**

"Uh, ahem, yes. Good afternoon Miss Crepe Cornelius, this is . . . the school, Monroe School. I hope everything is going well for you on this . . . Monday morning, afternoon. Monroe Middle School is calling to inform you that after due consideration, we feel we are going to have to go ahead and expel your son, Bongo. I repeat, Misses Cornelius, Bongo is expelled."

Horton hangs up and exhales, thinking that wasn't so bad. He looks at the next contact, picks up the phone, and begins to dial. Each ring that passes relieves Horton more and more. After the fourth, he is giddy, knowing the answering machine is about to take its course and permit him to again avoid a conversation. Horton hears the beep, and once again, he's on. Having already left one message, Horton feels he is now a pro.

"Hello, Miss Doinckus? This is the office of Monroe Middle School. We sure hope you are well on this Monday afternoon. This phone call is in regard to your son, Dirk, and his recent delinquent activities. After due consideration, we feel it will be best to let Dirk Doinckus go, and begin a new life path. Once again, we have exp—"

"Wait a minute. Hello?"

"Oh. I'm sorry," Horton stutters.

At this moment, Mr. Tray returns to the office from his lunch appointment. He has only been gone for about ten minutes.

"This is Delilah Doinckus, Dirk's mother. What is going on?"

Horton is paralyzed. Mr. Tray smiles at Horton and gives him a thumbs-up with his free hand. His other hand is holding a McDonalds bag.

"*Hello?!*"

"Yes, Misses Doinckus, excuse me. We've expelled your son."

Mr. Tray pauses at Horton's bluntness.

"*What the hell for?*"

"Um, you don't know?" worries Horton.

"*No. I don't know.*"

"Your son Dirk hasn't spoken to you about this?"

"*Dirk doesn't tell me shit!*"

"Has *no* one discussed Dirk's behavior with you?"

"*Who the hell is this? You better tell me what happened!*"

Horton motions for Mr. Tray to come help. Mr. Tray points to his bag of McDonalds. It's lunchtime.

"Dirk, uh. Your son . . . I forget, ma'am."

"*You forget why you're expelling my son?*"

"Yes. Well, actually. I wasn't told what he did."

"*You don't know why you're expelling my son?*"

Horton snaps his fingers, delirious.

Mr. Tray chews.

Horton SNAPS.

Mr. Tray points to the bag of fast food, meaning it's LUNCHTIME.

Horton gives up.

"You are correct, Delilah. I do not know. You might be able to take it up with—"

Mr. Tray hisses from the lunch table, "*Misses* Doinckus. Not *Delilah!* You are to call her *Misses* Doinckus!"

"*Who is this?*"

"I'm sorry?"

"*WHO. ARE. YOU!*"

"Misses Doinckus, please try to remain calm."

"*If you don't tell me who I am speaking with . . .*"

"Well Misses Doinckus, I'm Mr. Hagardy. A substitute," he shrivels.

"*A sub?!*"

"Right."

"*For* who?"

"Computer Lab Technician, ma'am. Today, for today."

"*WHAT?! Where is goddamned Mr. Tray?*"

"Well, actually, Mr. Tray has just—"

Mr. Tray is abruptly flailing his arms and whispering, "No! No! No! Not here! I'm NOT HERE!" Then he draws a line across his throat with his index finger.

"He is not here."

"*And the computer lab sub is expelling students?*"

"Right."

Mr. Tray is savoring chicken nuggets, jubilantly dumping meat rhombuses into little cartons.

"*I don't know what kind of office gerbil he got to do his dirty work, but you be sure to tell that wet noodle Mr. Tray that Dirk is not expelled and will be at school first thing tomorrow morning.*"

"I'll tell him at once."

There is a loud, messy click, signifying that Misses Doinckus has just spiked her phone down. Two phone calls remain, but Horton decides he's had enough.

"How are the phone calls coming?" asks Principal Tray in a fit of fried chicken glee.

"Great. Just made my last one."

"So. How does it feel to do some real work? I bet you didn't expect this when you woke up today. Try having those responsibilities every day."

"Thanks."

"I'll bet you're thinking, 'There's no way I could handle Mr. Tray's job.' Well I don't blame you because, personally, I don't think I could do *your* job. Everybody's different, you know. I need to be *doing* something. I need to make a difference. But that's just me."

Principal Tray's phone rings. He looks at the caller ID.

"Oops. It's the superintendent. Son of a gun always ends my lunch early. Well, Mr. Hagardy, if you'll excuse me, this is probably very important."

Principal Tray waits until Horton is nearly out of the room before he answers the phone: "Hey, Neil . . . ooooooh can't complain, another busy day on the choo choo . . . ."

Horton can't be gone quick enough.

When the lunch bell rings, he is eating his string cheese furiously. The next class enters the computer lab and begins its assignment, which appears to be a research project on various animals of the world. One student pulls up information on mountain gorillas. Another looks up chinchillas. Horton sees pictures of sharks. And beavers.

There is a knock at the door not even ten minutes into class. Mr. Tray steps into the room, accompanied by another man. Horton sighs. Promptly, Mr. Tray is in Horton's face.

"Hello, Mr. Hagardy, this is the superintendent of the district, Neil Floor. Say hello."

"Hello."

"Neil is here for a random inspection, just to see how things are going around school. Just to see if I'm doing my job. What do you think, Mr. Hagardy? Am I doing my job today?"

"Sure."

"So what are these kids working on?" Superintendent Floor asks Horton.

"An animal project."

"Have you been giving the students put-ups?" interrupts Mr. Tray and then nods at the superintendant.

"Huh?" Horton asks.

"Put-ups. Put-ups are the opposite of put-downs. They are phrases of positive reinforcement. I use them all the time. They keep the choo choo a runnin' smooth.

"You may be a visitor to Monroe, Mr. Hagardy, but as long as you're filling in for one of our instructors, you can abide by our methods."

Mr. Tray walks over to a student and nudges his shoulder.

"Name?" he whispers.

"Petey."

"PETEY!" announces Mr. Tray. "I like the way you are working quietly on your assignment! See, Mr. Hagardy, that's a put-up. Does your lesson plan not encourage put-ups?"

"No it doesn't."

Mr. Tray looks at Neil Floor uneasily.

"Are you sure that you looked through the lesson plan, Mr. Hagardy? Perhaps on the road to your two-hour nap this morning, you missed something. I remind all teachers to give put-ups, Mr. Hagardy."

Horton hands Principal *Tray Bien* a napkin with scribbles.

"This is my lesson plan."

Principal Tray is appalled. There is a malevolent silence in the computer lab that is fueled by Mr. Tray's distress and is ended when a child smears a fart into his plastic chair.

"I like the way Principal Tray just farted," sneers one kid under his breath, too inconspicuous to be spotted. Principal Tray labors to get to the bottom of the unsolved fart and the "put-up" that followed. No student confesses.

"*Control* them," Mr. Tray demands. He escorts Superintendent Floor around the room to inspect the projects. They pause in front of a child's computer screen, which is filled with shots of vaginas. Mr. Tray chokes on air. The child is terrified, as well, saying he was only looking for pictures for his project on beavers.

"*Solve* this," growls Mr. Tray at Horton as he herds Superintendent Floor out of the computer lab before he can be jeopardized by more treachery.

When the door closes, Horton says "Kid—I like how you pulled up all of those beavers in front of Mr. Tray."

Horton has just given a put-up.

The whole class gives the Beaver Kid a standing ovation. They are "putting him up," which is not to be confused with the physical reaction he likely had to a screen full of porn. Principal Tray Bien's departure is celebrated at length, essentially until the end of school.

The bell rings. Horton high fives everyone as they leave. It is 2:30. School is out. He won. Mr. Tray was foiled in front of his superior. Horton is on top of the world. He tiptoes into the office to sign out, intending to ignore Tray Bien's theories on putting in the full eight. He is ready to be gone from Monroe, and this time, forever.

From the back of the main office, Horton recognizes a voice, a voice he has learned to hate throughout the day. Principal Tray is locked in his office, having a good meaningless laugh with Superintendent Floor, so the voice is not his. It is elfish, whiny, and intrusive, like a child on the playground who invites herself to use everyone's toys.

Randi. She is in the back of the office, on the phone, fidgeting and rolling her eyes and punching digits in what seems to be a bout with debilitating confusion. Principal Tray has obviously enslaved her for the afternoon.

Horton signs his name in the book: Horton Hagardy. 2:45 p.m.

In the back, Randi grunts and says "Hello?" a few times then drops the receiver on the desk, an agonizing submission to technology. She has probably been assigned the afternoon shift of expelling Mr. Tray's students. One problem lies in her path, however. She can't dial a telephone. She could use a hand. Horton will not be donating his hand. He is about to leave when he accidentally makes eye contact with the disheveled hag.

"Do you get to leave?" she calls across the office.

"Huh?" asks Horton, initiating his flee.

"Are you leaving? We have to stay! The principal said we can't leave until four! Are you going to stay? I have to stay! I could really use your support!"

"I was, uh…doctor's appointment, lift weights," he mumbles

"Huh?"

"Pick up the kids, day care," he lies.

"YOU KNOW, I COULD REALLY USE SOME HELP!" persists fucking clueless Randi.

"Sssshhhhhhhh!" hisses Horton, giving Randi's strategy a try. But it's too late; the commotion has breached Principal Tray's conversation with Superintendent Floor. Tray Bien appears at his office door. He looks at Randi, who is sweating, possibly constipated with confusion, then he looks at Horton and smiles.

"Mr. Hagardy, it looks like your *colleague* is having a rough time. You wouldn't abandon a colleague in need, would you?"

"I could really use the support," Randi exhales. Horton would enjoy spraying her with a pressure hose.

"Of course you could. Who couldn't?" says Principal Tray Bien as if he's soothing a sixth grader who is struggling with her long division.

"Will you be staying to lend a hand to your colleague?"

Horton looks at the raggedy inept witch and swallows painfully the fact that she is his colleague—a woman with cancerous blather, a woman who cannot dial a phone. Horton and Randi—they are same. They are equal. They are substitutes.

"Is that going to work for you?" asks Principal Tray.

Horton sighs. He is not even thinking about the extra hour and a half of work—he couldn't care less about that now.

He nods, slowly, acceptingly.

"You'll thank me later. That's why I'm Tray Bien."

Fight or Flight

Middle School Gym

"Stay away from Mrs. Hovanov. Just stay the hell out of her way."

Horton receives this advice as he is led to the boys locker room of a middle school, an underground, mildew-insulated vault. With each step down the gymnasium staircase, natural light is lost to the dim flickering of a lamp. The sourness of old metal and sweat permeates as does the humidity of ever-unsettled dust. Horton feels like he is traipsing into the dingy den of a pirate ship, which is partially intriguing to him; since childhood, he has marveled the concept of pirates. Cobwebs and noodles of grit decorate the low ceilings of the locker room. Each step kicks up little typhoons of lint.

"Just down the hall and we'll be in the PE office," says the man escorting Horton, another PE teacher. "Home sweet home. Everything a guy needs. Fridge, magazines, some sodas, tunes, and our own private bathroom."

They descend further into what one might fear is a rogue civilization. Horton notices some form of non-potable water dripping from the ceiling into a widening puddle on the floor.

"You thirsty? Need a soda?" the man asks when they've entered the office.

"No, thanks."

"Gotta start the day off right."

He is holding a diet Crush, a little soft around the edges, not large, not small, not fat, not thin—he seems the type to prefer taking elevators up one floor, the type to think carrot debris in macaroni salad makes the side dish healthy.

"I'm going to check my fantasy football," he tells Horton. "Sorry, what's your name again?"

He reclines in his office chair as his computer yawns alive.

"Horton works for me."

"Ha! Funny name. I never introduced myself. Name's Brody Guyman, but everyone calls me Bro."

Horton registers this.

Bro. Guy. Man.

An older, heavyset man in a tracksuit enters, wading slowly toward the fridge.

"You're in for Bill today?" he asks. "Where's Bill?"

"He's got that big fantasy draft, remember?" says Bro, answering for Horton. "All day."

"That's right, that's right. He's got that today. The fantasy draft. All day. Hey, I'm Wally McFadden," he says to Horton. "Athletic director. You can call me McFaddy," he says, petting his torso.

"Your coworker is off for a fantasy football draft?" asks Horton.

"Oh yeah," says Brody. "If you take the game seriously, there's no other way."

"We get real competitive, Horton. Athletes always are," supports Wally.

"I had no idea. What sports do you guys play?" he asks.

They laugh.

"*Play?*" Brody relishes.

"We got a jokester on our hands," says Wally.

Brody has risen from the computer and entered the personal bathroom, closing the door behind him with a magazine in hand, leaving nothing of his intentions up for speculation.

Wally has opened the fridge. "Horton, right? You need a soda?"

"No thanks."

Wally grabs one for himself and begins trading sips between a mug of coffee and the cola.

"Anything you need, fridge, magazine, sodas. You'll see, we live it up down here. It's like our own little bunker that no one remembers to check on. The only thing you gotta watch out for is Mrs. Hovanov. Just do yourself a big favor and stay the *hell* out of her way."

"Who is this woman?" Horton asks.

"A gym teacher, on the girl's side. A real twat, Horton."

"Ah *hell!*" barks Brody from the can over some of his other noises. "Just remembered we gotta renew our CPR certificates today!"

"*Tits!*" snarls Wally.

The bell rings. Middle school children rush in to the locker room. Their energy at eight in the morning is phenomenal.

"Say it ain't so!" cries Brody. "Is it too late to call in sick?"

"Another day another dollar," Wally groans, at which point he lumbers out of the office and into the sea of piranhas that is the boy's locker room. He then blows his whistle like Dizzy Gillespie, cheeks exploding, neck veins inflated.

"HEY! GET DRESSED AND *GET UPSTAIRS!*"

The mayhem of the children continues unaltered.

"HEY! SHUT YOUR FRICKIN' MOUTHS!"

Wally's bellows are raising the noise level with which the children must compete to be heard. He squeezes himself between kids, patrolling the room as they dress.

"Hey! You got gum? Better not be chewin' gum!"

Horton has no idea what he should be doing. Wally has disappeared behind a barrier of lockers.

"SPIT OUT YOUR FRICKIN' *GUM*!"

Horton shudders.

"WHO'S GOT GUM!" thunders Brody, who has healed from his digestive tribulations to aid Wally in this early morning gum raid. Horton shuffles about, feeling pressure to contribute to the crackdown, so he walks around, attempting an alpha-male grimace to compliment the behaviors of Brody and Wally. Once it is established that no children have gum, the three men return to the office. Class begins at 9:05. It is 9:05. Brody appears to be on a fantasy football website.

"You do fantasy football, Horton?" asks Brody.

"Can't say that I do."

"Wow."

For the next ten minutes, Brody and Wally relax in chairs and deliberate on strategy—who to play, who to trade, who's injured, who's been "looking up."

Horton checks his watch, confused.

"Are we supposed to go upstairs?" he asks. "For class?"

"Is it about that time?" Wally groans.

"Yep," says Brody. "Hell."

On their way out, Brody fills Horton in on the complexities of his job.

"I'm going to give you a sack of basketballs, and your kids are going to play around."

Horton awaits further responsibilities.

"That's it."

"You don't want me to have them do a few layup drills? Chest passes? Nothing like that? Jumping jacks?"

"*What?*"

"I thought maybe you wanted me to go through some warm-ups."

"HA!" raves Brody. "Layups?"

"We got a go-getter on our hands," says Wally, painfully making his way up the stairs. "Goddamn my knees."

After taking roll, Horton takes his kids to the basketball court where he, per his orders, opens the sack of basketballs. The children dribble them and occasionally shoot. For an hour. The peak of fitness is reached when a girl chases a boy in circles to recapture her stolen cell phone. Beyond that, the only difference between Horton's students and a herd of cattle is the noise they make to protest their mind-rotting boredom. The morning fog is wrathful, rolling horizontally across the courts like the dewy air found in pastoral images of Scotland.

"This suuuuuuuuuuuuucks," the children mourn.

"Can we go insiiiiiiiiiiiiiiiiiiiiide?"

"It's like, rainnnniiiiinnnnnnnnnnnnnnng."

"We're going to get siiiiiiiiiiiiiiick."

This is like one of those exhibits at the San Francisco Zoo where the animals are quarantined outside in the morning permafrost with nothing more than a bowl of drinking water and an uninspiring rubber ball. Horton remembers being in middle school and running around because it was actually fun. He sucked at basketball, but that didn't stop him from playing. He barely understood football, but it was still fun to catch a pass and avoid getting the flag ripped from his waist. He remembers classmates being active; if they weren't, they ran as punishment. They essentially had the option to run, or run.

"You know, studies have proven that movement of any kind can warm the body," suggests Horton.

Students stare at him.

"This guy suuuuuuuuuuuuuucks," moos one student.

In the distance, somewhere in the fog, Horton hears the echoes of Brody accusing a student of harboring gum. Visibility is getting worse. There seems to be a shadowy bulge lurching in the courts. Horton squints. The bulge drifts in the fashion of a gluttonous sea bass in the depths of its murky pond. It disappears, swallowed by the fog only to reappear closer, huger. Then it ripples away.

"You guys see that thing?" Horton frets to his kids.

"See what?"

"I'm not sure, it went away."

Horton squints more. A whistle tweets somewhere, signifying the end of class. The children flee to the locker room.

"There! Wait, there it is! Look!" Horton exclaims, but the students have dissolved.

The colossal lump seems levitated, observing Horton with motionless curiosity.

"Hello?" asks Horton. "Are you . . . something?"

The slab wafts away. Horton walks through the drapery of atmosphere, sticking his hands out before each step as though blindfolded.

"Jesus," he sighs upon rediscovering the campus. In the office, Brody and Wally are exploring the possibilities of more soda.

"Hey. How about that weather out there, Horton?" Brody asks.

"I could barely see the kids, but they didn't do much, I'm almost certain."

"Man they suck," Brody sympathizes.

"I think I was seeing something, too. Like a huge fish, or some drifting tree stump, or a VW bug sliding around in neutral."

"That was Mrs. Hovanov," Brody says. "She does that when it's foggy, spies on other teachers, makes sure they're sticking to curriculum. A real twat, Horton."

"Was I not following curriculum?"

"It's gym, man. Kids move around. What curriculum?" Wally mumbles through reading glasses and coffee steam. "Been doin' this for forty years."

The voice of reason has been issued. Brody tells Horton not to worry, reminding him that he's got it easy.

"At least you don't have to get CPR certified today."

Horton got certified for CPR once to coach little league. The process took thirty seconds.

"How'd you like to give CPR to Mrs. Hovanov?" sneers Wally.

"Ha! BRUTAL!" Bro celebrates. "Absolutely brutal!"

Hearing of Mrs. Hovanov's mist prowls has left Horton paranoid, so for the next few periods he is firmer with his students about keeping active and at least appearing to achieve some level of fitness. He frequently looks over his shoulder and wonders if the images he thinks he's seeing are all in his mind, or in fact the gym teacher's huge spying ass.

Each period, the mist is thicker, gooier, more intrusive of clear sight and thought. Balls are bouncing around Horton; he sees none. His entire class could very well be mooning him from five feet away or conspiring to assassinate him. He wouldn't know. At the sound of the lunch bell, the students do not return the balls, leaving Horton to track them down in this arena of apparitions and mind tricks. At this moment, Horton wishes he was a submarine, or a dolphin, or any other entity with sonar.

Following a spooky repo of gym basketballs, Horton finds his way back to the locker room. Brody is going through a magazine, eating some rectangular, microwavable item. Wally is staring at the computer screen, ruing the fact that he must renew his CPR certification.

"Who even needs CPR here? Who's choking in our gym? Nobody's chewin' any gum!" he fusses, then begins his test.

Wally whizzes through it and gets every question wrong. Brody assures Wally that the website lets you retake it as many times as needed because it *only* cares about your money. Wally heeds this advice and is awarded a CPR certificate directly after entering his credit card information. Brody does the same, and both have renewed their CPR certifications in ten minutes.

"Oh. HA! Uh oh, McFaddy. We need to take a survey."

"A *survey?*"

"The district wants to know how it can improve."

"Can this lunch *get* any worse?"

Brody opens the survey.

"Horton, you a smart guy? What'd you do in college?"

"I did poetry."

"Ha! Oh man. What for?"

For this reason, Horton hates being asked that question unless in the company of other emasculating-degree holders.

"I was interested in writing poems. Haven't been able to publish much, though."

"Hell," soothes Brody. "Economy's tough right now. Goes in cycles. It will come around."

Horton passes on the opportunity to tell Brody that a poet's success is unlinked to the state of the economy.

"Well, maybe you can help us with these surveys, Horton. The shit never makes sense to us. Number one. Get a load of this. 'I am confident my district is competitive and committed to its advances and efforts to bolster functioning and cultivating foundations of scholastic stimulation within the district.'"

"What the hell?" asks Wally.

"If I'm not mistaken, the district wants to know if it has put you in a position to be a successful teacher," Horton says.

"Here's the choices," says Brody. "Very confident, sometimes confident, undecided, and unconfident."

"Unconfident," grumbles McFaddy. "Do unconfident."

"HA!" agrees Bro.

"Next."

"'Needs and priorities of students are fulfilled by implemented curriculum and necessary bi-annual budget-funneling adjustments. Certain, rather certain, conflicted, distinctly suspicious.' Horton, what's this one asking?"

"Sounds like . . . they want to know if you're in a position to be a good teacher."

"Oh. I am *distinctly* suspicious," says Wally.

"Ha!" Brody rejoices.

"Next."

"'Targeted areas of focus and improvement are narrow, concise and reasonably attainable within set instructional guidelines of district education protocol.'"

"We're gym teachers for christsake!" cries Wally.

"It's the same question."

"Screw these idiots!"

Brody selects the option "in vigorous disagreement."

For the remainder of lunch, Brody and Wally are flummoxed by the survey. When the bell rings, students flood inside to get changed. Wally unleashes another manhunt for gum chewers. All the kids are soaked, which means that sheets of mist that draped the campus earlier have now matured into heavy rain. This calls for indoor activities, which, according to Brody, means packing seventy kids into a gym and engaging them.

"It can get zany."

Horton is asked to patrol the gym as students enter to make

sure they sit on their assigned numbers instead of engaging in riots, which is what they will do if left unmonitored. Students begin to trickle into the gym and, upon seeing Horton, become lawless.

"Please sit on your number. Excuse me, students, please sit on your numbers," tries Horton; he is as good as invisible. More students enter and join the mutiny. Horton attempts to contain them, but as a general rule of thumb, thirteen-year-olds do not respect people without authority. By definition, Horton has no authority.

One kid has just heaved another into the matted part of the floor. They celebrate. There is more than one game of wrestle-tag. A girl has just done a cartwheel into a boy's nuts. With the coming of more and more gym students, the anarchy snowballs and rises in volume.

"Boys and girls, please find your—"

A whistle harpoons the eardrums of everyone in the gym. The noise is debilitating—a tazer to the auditory senses, a killer whale auditioning for lead soprano. Children nearest the whistle are stunned into paralysis. The blower of the whistle is clear now that the children are moving on the floor like ants sprayed with Raid. She takes the whistle out of her mouth. Layers of fat compile around her skull like expanding ripples in a pond of pudding. Below her chin swings a cow udder. A few warts push from within layers of her facial flesh like half-smoked, hairy cigarettes tucked away for later. She seems to be wearing a sea-green shower curtain for clothes. This is Mrs. Hovanov, Horton deduces.

She plods toward him at the speed of the spirit that haunted him in the fog.

"Will you be facilitating the rainy day activity?" she asks.

"Not that I know of."

"So I have to do it again?"

"I haven't been told much about what I'm supposed to be doing."

"I'm the only one that teaches or does a goddamned thing."

For a moment, Horton amuses himself with the thought of naive children approaching this woman for aerobic instruction, not knowing that she, a gym teacher, cannot physically do anything.

Mrs. Hovanov, I'm having trouble with my tennis serve. Can you show me the proper mechanics?

Or:

Mrs. Hovanov, I seem to be missing all of my layups. Would it be possible for you to demonstrate the proper form?

Or:

Mrs. Hovanov, can you show me how to jump rope? Jumping jack? Climb rope? Sprint? Field a groundball? Somersault?

"Excuse me," invades Mrs. Hovanov, "could you control these students instead of grinning? Substitutes are typically asked to do more than have a heartbeat, despite your hopes."

Horton can hardly see past her; she is eclipsing his view of the gym. She is panoramic. It is impossible for this woman to have ordered a salad since the late seventies, yet she is a tenured advocate of fitness and healthy life choices for San Francisco's youth.

"YOU CHEWIN' GUM!? IN *MY* GYM!?"

Here they come, waddling in tandem.

"GO SIT ON YOUR FRICKIN' NUMBER, BOZO! HEY, COCONUT-HEAD! SPIT IT OUT, OR *GET OUT!*"

Horton watches them in action, wondering what students think of them. Middle school is an interesting time. At thirteen, one begins the process of budding muscles and mustaches and breasts and menstrual cycles, and with these additions come psychological renovations, leaving children with swagger, defiance, and flawless insight. If they understand algebra, they've surpassed Galileo. If they've read *Harry Potter*, they need read no more; they *get* literature. They are all smarter than their parents.

But with this revolutionary wisdom impregnating them at the pace of their sprouting whiskers, they also believe when they are taught that marijuana causes car wrecks. Yes, adolescence is a time of great physical and cerebral triumphs, but it is also a time of naivety, which means they may see nothing odd about having gluttonous instructors of fitness. *Irony*, despite their mastery of literature, is not a term they will come to fully understand until later.

They're too busy being kids to speculate about the legitimacy of the adults in their lives. They don't *care*. They've got baseball practices and drum lessons and gymnastic meets and science projects and sleepovers and secret crushes and intrusive parents and favorite movies and heroes. Every kid has heroes, dreams. Horton used to have them, he remembers. When he was too young to know any better, he used to roll around in the backyard playing shootem' up by himself, thinking he was a big brave army guy. Later, he wanted to be a baseball player, a slugging first basemen for the Oakland Athletics just like Mark McGwire; who *didn't* want to be Big Mac?

Now, Horton is an adult, and that is the extent of his title— an adult. He has all the time in the world to be cynical, to doubt people and compare himself to others just like everyone else. He works, like many, a job which he'd never considered, a job that makes him feel forgotten. Even Wally and Brody— *and* Mrs. Hovanov—have the pleasure of playing a role in memories. The one thing Horton can hang his hat on is his daily opportunity to be around children, for children live vivaciously and act as though they will never grow up, and never be forgotten. If there is something to be taken from his forgettable job, his forgettable days, and the forgettable truth that growing up makes you smaller in this world, it is being around children.

"Excuse me. Do you have the ability to control your students?" persists Mrs. Hovanov. "Or have those two slugs taught you the art of being useless?"

"HEY, DONKEY BRAINS! ZIP IT AND SIT DOWN!" echoes Brody from a nook in the gym.

Mrs. Hovanov blows her whistle and invites students to sit for roll call or be expelled. Then she huffs over to Brody.

"Here we go," he says.

"Brody, why don't *you* organize the rainy day activity for the students today?"

"You gotta be . . . *again?*" he snorts.

"Psh," scoffs Wally in support, followed by a *psh* from Brody.

"Call me *Bro*."

After attendance, Brody disappears into a side door and emerges with a basketball.

"This is some *bull*," he says to himself, then explains his activity to the full gym: there will be one basketball game, on one standard basketball court, involving all seventy students—something to the tune of thirty versus thirty, with a few subs of course. Brody and Wally join their two classes for one team, feigning intent to "team-coach." They are presently chuckling about an irrelevant matter. Horton is stranded with Mrs. Hovanov, who is busy hating her colleagues on the other side of the court. Brody ushers the basketball through the sea of children toward half court for the "tipoff."

A nerd on Brody's team has been selected to oppose a kangaroo-faced barbarian from Horton's squad at half court. Brody lifts the ball into the air. The man-child jumps and swats, hitting nothing. Then the ball comes down and bounces off the malnourished nerd's head; he crumbles. The game has begun, and already it sounds like a heated labor union strike. When someone tries to follow the rules—say, dribble—the ball either bounces off of someone's shins or is savagely burglarized like a loaf of bread during famine. Everyone is traveling. Children spew unorthodox half court shots not to score but to avoid being tackled for the ball. Layups are impossible. Passing is dangerous. Waves of movement reveal students who are lying on the floor, trampled. Cannibalism is brewing. Knowing who is on whose team is incalculable. A small Asian girl looks down to find the ball in her hand. She produces the same look of terror as a soldier who sees he is holding his spleen; she shoots it and is promptly stuffed by someone. The ball ends up right back in her hands. She heaves it again to divert all pursuers of the ball. Her shot is once again stuffed. This time the ball returns to her face and flattens her nose. She disappears, swallowed into people. The ball pops up randomly as though it has been stuck in the depths of the sea and has forcefully surged to the surface. From there, it goes for a ride along the fingertips of the high-voltage children like a crowd surfer.

Mrs. Hovanov is boiling, hissing soliloquies of all-encompassing bitterness. There comes a point when some kids begin stacking on one another in a makeshift pyramid toward the hoop, the goal being to pass the ball to the highest kid for a slam dunk. Much like ancient Egypt, there are many casualties in the erecting of this pyramid; fingers are sprained, lips are split, wrists are twisted, teeth are chipped. Naturally, Wally and Brody can't get enough. They chuckle and point, directing each other to this excess of bloopers. Children are approaching Wally and Brody in need of medical aid; however, Brody and Wally wave them off and point them to Mrs. Hovanov, who throws her hands up in a fit.

"*You* walk to them and see why they can't treat the injured. It's *their* goddamned game," Mrs. Hovanov snarls at Horton.

Horton walks to the other side, acting as messenger.

"Can you believe that woman?" Brody bursts.

"A real twat, Horton," says Wally, "like we've been saying all along."

"They don't pay us enough for this, eh McFaddy?"

The children are aching, bleeding, fading.

"What should I tell her?" Horton asks.

"Send them to the counselors, for christsake," says Wally. "I can't be seen touching any kids. Not with all the lawsuits floating around. You know my buddy over at Jack London Middle School?"

Horton wonders if that is even a question.

"He got fired for teachin' some little jerk how to throw a baseball, grabbing his arm and givin' him proper technique. Said he was reaching for his yoohoo. Unbelievable. Then, did you hear about that other guy, over there at Willie Stargell Elementary—got fired just for being out on the playground with a kid, not even touching him, just standing out there after school. Said he was looking "suspiciously hungered." Had to leave the district, pack up his whole family, and go somewhere else. Sorry man, I'm not taking any risks. I'm not getting the boot because some little bastard blows the whistle on me when I'm trying to put a Band-Aid on him, telling everyone I was reaching for his Willy Wonka!"

"No way. Not with kids wavin' the flag about their ding-dongs," supports Brody.

"Everyone's putting together tales about their Tootsie Rolls."

"The girls with their na-nas," Brody belabors.

Horton walks back to tell Mrs. Hovanov that the current

shortage of medical aid is a result of teachers *saving* their jobs. She shoots her whistle and storms to the middle of the court, shoving children the way hippopotamuses shove water when performing cannonballs. The injured are sent as a limping caravan to the counseling office where there are no ice packs or first aid kits.

"THIS GAME IS OVER!" she announces. "SIT DOWN ON YOUR NUMBERS, SHUT YOUR MOUTHS, OR FIND NEW SCHOOLS. NOW LISTEN! WE'RE GOING TO DO A DIFFERENT GAME. PAY ATTENTION TO THE INSTRUCTIONS. I'M ONLY TELLING YOU ONCE!"

Mrs. Hovanov introduces a "team-building" activity, which she learned at a professional development day.

"Since I'm the only one that even *goes* to those damned things," she mutters. "I'll tell you right now, the materials for this game are expensive, and fragile. You're going to treat them with respect, you're going to treat them with care, or you're going to have Mommy and Daddy find. You. A. New. School!"

At that, the unceremonious beast disappears into the equipment room and emerges with several thin colored ribbons, some plastic capes, and Styrofoam balls. She explains the complex rules of the game once, and only once, after which the rules are clear to no one. Horton is certain that Mrs. Hovanov is unclear of the rules herself.

When the kids are unleashed to play the befuddling "team-builder," pure enthusiasm shreds Mrs. Hovanov's materials into confetti. The gym floor quickly resembles New Orleans during Mardi Gras. To salvage what remains, Mrs. Hovanov lunges into the mayhem, her gargantuan tits flailing sideways like ottomans gone haywire. She screams, *STOP! STOP! STOP!* but the children can't seem to be calmed. Mrs. Hovanov is mid-court, waving children out of her way, scooping scraps and

Styrofoam into her bust. With the floor so slippery from paper shreds, she slips and systematically tips over, sprawled, beached.

"Ha!" echoes Brody across the gym.

Wally rolls his eyes. Students are mumbling, but the gym has, for the most part, gone awkwardly silent. A wretched neigh then billows into the gym air. Children are distancing themselves from the noise, revealing Mrs. Hovanov's carcass. Her beckons are gurgling and hideous like the noises of overheating and disease-entrenched wild animals. The warts embedded in her throat are twitching like baby fingers reaching for a stranger's beard. The children widen the circle that surrounds her. Brody and Wally look at one another quizzically, having managed to stifle their amusement for the time being. Both are whispering to each other, shrugging. Mrs. Hovanov's condition worsens, as indicated by a crescendo in her opus of agony. She begins demanding CPR, suddenly certain that the injury she has sustained will be alleviated by a violent puncturing of her windpipe.

Students head toward Brody and Wally, informing them, if they haven't heard already, that CPR may be needed. Wally and Brody whisper more, exchanging confidentialities, assessing the predicament, and making important decisions as the adults in command. They nod in agreement.

If Horton is not mistaken, Brody has just whispered something about "paperwork."

Wally nods approvingly and whispers something about "soda."

The two disappear into the woodwork, presumably executing whatever escape they've just ad-libbed to avoid oral contact with their colleague. Even if they were somehow feeling responsible, there is no way they could ever save a life with

CPR, based on their lunchtime failures. They are probably just sharp enough to deduce that no one *needs* CPR if they are able to consciously request it.

Students are now looking at Horton, the next in command now that Brody and Wally have exempted themselves. Mrs. Hovanov has managed to sit up onto her two generous ham hocks to fondle her booboo and command CPR some more.

This situation has more than exceeded the realm of folly. Mrs. Hovanov is launching a tirade on Horton, the worm-like qualities of substitute teachers, and the impotent infrastructure of all living men. Horton's pulpy fight or flight juices are arriving at the scene, as it seems he has precisely two options: withstand her for a doughy voyage into utter vileness, or flee. Flee as did the others, flee as he should.

Stay away from Mrs. Hovanov. Just stay the hell out of her way, they said.

Horton is a sub; CPR is not his job. Nothing is his job; his job *is* nothing! Better fit than any is Horton to avoid responsibility, for the very nature of his job is to be forgotten—to show up, serve a futile purpose, and then leave, never to be remembered. Every fiber of his occupation is saturated in the notion of the easy way out. All he needs to do is walk. People might say the substitute wasn't there, but that news will pale in comparison to Wally and Brody, the real teachers, ducking out mere hours after getting recertified for CPR. Horton, per usual, will be just a back story, an incomplete thought, a faceless bystander in the background of people's recollections of *remember-that-time-when-Hovanov-fell-down-in-gym-and-laid-there-pretending-to-die?* Horton, the substitute, will play no role in that. He has no role, in general. He is expendable, and, above all else, forgettable.

Goddamnit, thinks Horton, as Mrs. Hovanov huffs and snarls.

He wonders if it will always be this way. Is his historical ghostliness doomed to prevail?

Horton can walk, like he does at the end of every day, and continue to be forgotten. Or—he can do something, something that students will dissect and laugh and cringe and sneer about long into their adult lives, something that absolutely no one will comprehend, something that no one in their right mind could possibly do without being treated afterwards for post-traumatic stress. But it is something no one will ever forget.

Some people hit walk-off homeruns in their lives.

Some people get elected president.

Some people write best sellers.

Some people risk their lives to save others.

Some people are revolutionary in the advancements of certain races and marginalized factions of society.

Horton isn't so lucky. He will not be remembered for such tremendous feats, and if he doesn't do anything about it, he will not be remembered by anyone, for anything. Look at her over there, Horton thinks as Mrs. Hovanov makes the noises of a warthog with a sinus infection. Horton can't believe he is about to drape his mouth over hers. He will subject himself to her breath, the particles of lunch left in her teeth, the salt-pocked slab that is her tongue.

Mrs. Hovanov's screams are now acoustic carnage. Wally and Brody are likely downstairs, enjoying a soda while comparing farts. Soon the bell will ring and students will leave. Horton's window of opportunity is closing. He can be, or be forgotten. Stand or walk. Fight or fly. Maybe this will be the turning point he's needed, the moment that tells him if he can do this, he can do anything, and be anyone. This will be what changes Horton's life for good, sets him in an entirely new direction.

Horton begins walking. Never has he stood so tall in his

stride. His body is pulsing and tingling with life and purpose. This will be a new beginning for Horton. It's happening. His eyes are closed.

"Where are you going?" belches Mrs. Hovanov.

Children are watching, some confused, some curious, some unsurprised. And Horton doesn't stop walking.

"HEY!" she grovels from half court.

By the time Horton is downstairs, the bell has rung. Children fill up the locker room and begin changing out of their gym clothes, speaking animatedly about what just transpired.

"Did you see the look on that sub's face?" they say. "And he just jetted."

"*So* funny."

"How crazy would it have been if he actually gave her CPR?"

"*So* crazy."

When the room clears, Horton returns to the office. Brody is on the computer, addressing his fantasy football team under the counsel of Wally.

"So how'd it go up there?" asks Brody as he clicks around with the mouse.

"Never got that far, I guess," Horton replies.

"Who can blame you? Hey, what've we been telling you all along? Stay the hell away from her, right?"

"Horton," Wally says, "you need a soda?"

Horton is tired, slumped in his chair. It is fatiguing to feel worthless, forgotten. He looks at the soda in the man's hand, blurred by tiny droplets of condensation. Horton cannot deny its alluring qualities, the hope of being quenched, somehow.

"I guess," Horton concedes.

"Ha!" Brody sounds, though it is unclear if he is referring to Horton, or his computer.

Bobbing Away

College and Career

"Education is our passport to the future, for tomorrow belongs to the people who prepare for it today."
—Malcolm X.

Horton feels he can learn much about a teacher from the posters and quotes hanging in the classroom. For instance, San Francisco Giants World Series banners or Muhammad Ali posters suggest young teachers of somewhat competitive spirit, perhaps ex-college athletes. Posters of Sally Ride, Eleanor Roosevelt, or Susan B. Anthony suggest a teacher whose ideals are sprinkled with feminist zest. Teachers of progressive and against-the-grain thought tend to display Albert Einstein, Mark Twain (Einstein's biological twin), Rosa Parks, Gandhi, or Marlon Brando to name a few. Shakespeare is erected when teachers can think of nothing else to put up.

Horton doesn't know what to make of this Malcolm X quote. It is simple, basic, and about education. Such quotes are usually in elementary schools next to cartoon drawings of caterpillars reading books and endorsements for calcium-fortified milk. But Horton is at a high school today, and by the time kids are in high school, such quotes are so overused that they work reversely, motivating children to take bong rips and fail classes out of spite. Horton wonders what high school demographic this quote suits. He has no idea what he is teaching today; the phone call this morning seemed to tactfully withhold that information.

"There is a substitute assignment available for: high... school...classroom...teacher," the automated voice droned. Horton took the job, despite his suspicion that its vagueness was meant to prevent subs from learning how awful the job was. Horton did not care; he was desperate. It was the first day back from San Francisco's winter break, the annual two-week period of financial and psychological trauma for substitutes. Unlike regular teachers, when there is no school, subs are not paid, making winters and summers times of intense and imaginative thriftiness. Horton walks outrageous distances to save gas, he sleeps in polar wear to leave the heater off, he lights candles, he eats so much string cheese, among other sub-dollar snacks that, by the end, some medical attention isn't a bad idea. So this morning, he needed the work, no matter what, and now he wonders what's in store.

"*THAT'S* HOW COME YOU A CRUSTY BITCH! *AND* YOU GOT A CAMEL TOE. *NOW* WHAT?!"

Horton's thoughts have been forced into hasty resolve. The source of the commotion stampedes into the room; Horton flinches.

An administrator has followed the girl.

"I wish you wouldn't yell at me and call me names," says the administrator.

"It ain't callin' names, it's stating *facts*."

"I'm your counselor. You are expected to speak to adults with respect."

"Freedom of speech, *BIIIIIIIIIITTTTTCHH!*"

The counselor walks away during the girl's appalling

reminder of her rights, but not before Horton is able to confirm that the counselor *does* have a camel toe. Now he and this girl are the only two in the room.

"You the sub?" she asks, then smacks gum loud enough for an Olympian to think the race has begun.

"Yes."

"What we s'posed to call you?"

"Mr. Hagardy."

The girl is opening a bag of spicy Cheetos, a unanimous breakfast choice among San Francisco's urban scholars, Horton's observed.

"Your name *bootsy*," she accuses—bootsy being synonymous with lower tier. "If that was my last name, I wouldn't never have kids."

"Oh."

"You look like a microwave-pizza-eatin', no-sex-havin'-ass bum. What, you live in a shoe box?"

These insults are happening too quickly for Horton to process; by the time she's moved on to more, Horton is still wondering how this girl knows that he microwaves pizzas. More students enter, exchanging vulgarities. Horton is sitting at the teacher's desk, looking through the lesson plan as one kid after another directs at him the inquiry "Who da *fuck's* this?" Horton feels he is being noted the way all things are noted by rabid Dobermans.

The lesson plan says that he will be teaching College and Career, a class geared toward helping students thrive after high school. The class is beginning a unit on job interviews—attire, attitude, and execution. Horton's assignment is to go over a worksheet on interview procedure and then engage the students in mock interviews. Horton is assured that the class size is small and that the school's resident motivator will be there to help smooth things along; he knows the kids and is acquainted with the "structure and routine of the class."

Once the bell rings, there are six kids present—a small class, indeed. Two of them quickly hack onto a website and begin playing games. One game involves the repeated process of slingshotting animals into barricades of lumber, another is about launching someone from skyscraper to helicopter to skyscraper ala some urban trapeze act. When the character falls, he dies with gory squirts and carrot-stick-cracking bone noises to clear up any doubt that the character is dead. The children play this game with the mindlessness of assembly line workers.

Presumably, the resident motivator has arrived, a meek and slender man; no belt is working harder than his. His nose is a chess bishop coated in flesh, thin and bumpy. He and Horton shake hands—more specifically, Horton grabs the man's hand and ripples it. He introduces himself as Bjorsh, but leaves Horton the option of addressing him as Hamster.

"It's what the kids call me, so it might be best for you to stick with that. Any deviation from 'the routine' with these kids can get ugly quick."

Horton agrees to call the resident motivator by his preferred title, then moves forward with the day's agenda.

"Boys, can you get off the computers," Horton begins. "It's time for class, and I'm certain those are meant for research and classwork."

"These is *educational* games," a boy argues.

"That's not possible."

Somewhere else in the room, bags of spicy Cheetos squeal open. Those who aren't playing computer games have their ears buried in satellite-dish-sized headphones. Rap lyrics, which are all rhymed details of unspeakable sexual conquests, are being recited. The students bob their heads to the beat, bob their heads like pigeons strutting about. In an attempt to end this, Horton tries giving the most mundane disclaimer a substitute can give—a mistake, in nearly every case:

"I know I'm a substitute, guys, but I'm still a teacher, and I expect you to act just like you would if your regular teacher was here."

What Horton doesn't know, and what he would certainly benefit *from* knowing, is that students take such a statement to mean: "I am a powerless, sniveling troll. I know it, you know it, and I'm bitter about it."

Horton shifts his weight, then chokes on some air, which feeds the awkwardness in the room. The students are salivating at Horton's unease.

"You know what I'd do?"

Hamster has leaned in to offer some counsel.

"I'd make a deal with them. I'd tell them they had until you were done with attendance to finish their game, or to finish their music. That way they feel like they're getting something out of it."

Horton heeds Hamster's idea, and the kids carry forth in a way that suggests they would have kept fucking around with or without this "deal." Horton looks at the roll sheet, reads the first name, looks away to let his eyes process the data, and returns to it to see if what he just read was real.

"Sir Prize Bailey?" he calls.

"Here," calls a boy from the computer.

Horton stares at the next one: Mah'Star. The class is hungry for a mispronunciation.

"Ma Star Caldwell? Ma. Star."

"*Master*," says Mah'Star.

"Your name is Master?"

"Yeuh."

Mah'Star looks like he plays a position in football that involves putting opponents in the hospital, so that is Horton's last question on the matter.

The next name is Yurheyenez Collins.

"Yer hayah-nez Collins?" Sounds Muslim. Perhaps eastern European. "Is Yuur-hay-yeenz here?"

"Your Highness."

It's the girl who accurately accused Horton of eating microwave pizzas and being unintentionally abstinent. Her hair is died red, gum exploding.

"Your Highness."

Next is Rolls Royce Garrison III, who's wearing a sweatshirt big enough to double as a helicopter gurney for a hippo. Following Rolls Royce, there is –anette, who scolds Horton for his ignorance of punctuation; her name is not Anette, but *Dash*anette.

The next name is Abcd'n Lofton.

"Oh boy," Horton frets, then squints. Yes, he's read it correctly. This is a notable affair.

"I may need some assistance," quakes Horton.

"Ab-kuddin?" he neighs. "Ub-caddy-in?"

"Obsidian," states a boy. "Obsidian."

"Oh, yes."

In this case, Horton is delighted by this name's defiance of English language protocol, and the wit of its alphabetic performance.

"What's *yo* name?" interjects –anette.

"My name?" Horton asks.

"Yea. We ain't know *yo* name yet."

"It's Horton."

The students riot, exceptionally, over the name.

"Dr. Seuss-ass little elf!"

"Wart-growin, moldy-sock-wearin', brussel-sprout-buyin'."

"Dodge-Colt-drivin', hair-losin', booty-ass-morning-breath-havin'."

Horton feels as though his (evidently balding) hair is blowing back like a scientist at a nuclear testing site as these children verbally carpet-bomb his name. Furthermore, he wonders how the *hell* these kids could have known that he drives a Dodge Colt!

"Now that we've established a head count, shall we move on to the lesson plan?"

Horton reminds his students that he is finished with roll, which means that they must log off the computers, put their headphones away, and stow away their food. This includes spicy Cheetos, a regulation they will not stand for. As a union, they protest that they cannot learn on empty stomachs, citing a statistic, likely from a useless assembly on nutrition, that students learning on an empty stomach are twice as likely to forget than those who have eaten. Horton mentions that it is their responsibility as students to eat breakfast before school— ideally something that is not spicy Cheetos. —anette identifies Horton's dismissal of spicy Cheetos as racist, and that's the end of that conversation, for there is nothing more mortifying to a teacher in the San Francisco public school system than being accused of racism. Horton has heard too many tales of teachers unknowingly making inferences to cultural habits or preferences and waking up to job-terminating lawsuits. —anette realizes what she has accomplished, and now the entire class eats spicy Cheetos with renewed vigor.

Hamster leans in to donate more counsel. "It might be best to just let them eat."

"Okay fine. Let's get to work. You guys have had a little free time, you've had a little breakfast, now Hamster is going to pass out a worksheet and we're going to move on to the business of job interviews—the cornerstone of success in our competitive society. Your first impression is remembered forever, and can certainly determine your success. More than often, job interviews are your first impression."

There is no positive response to this. Rolls Royce III's sweatshirt is swallowing him like a turtle shell. Yurheyenez is discoursing on her already-infallible job interview skills—skills that need no further refining. Horton asks Sir Prize to take his hat off and to put his rap music away, at which point Sir Prize accuses Horton of racially profiling him for assuming that his music is rap, though the volume of the music deems the genre undisputable. Fear and frustration are causing Horton's eyelids to flutter like an injured bird, and the day is still young. Is it possible that Horton *is* being racist? Is his job presently in jeopardy?

Hamster steps in to restore ease—and equity—to the room, telling Sir Prize that he will cut him a deal: he can continue to wear his hat in class as long as he puts his music away for a while. Sir Prize compromises with *that* compromise, sliding the headphones off of his head so that they're hanging from his neck. He does not, however, turn the music off, and so now the headphones are projecting the songs, with lyrics of masochistic foreplay, like mini speakers. Horton peers at Hamster, who seems pleased by the compromise Sir Prize has just made.

"Dashanette," will you please begin reading with the first employment disclaimer on the worksheet?"

"No."

"What?"

"I ain't feel good."

"You've seemed fine all morning," Horton says, his blood

pressure reaching the peaks of Machu Picchu.

"I ain't had breakfast. I got a headache. I'm goin' to the Wellness Center."

What the *hell* is a Wellness Center? wonders Horton. Has she just made this up? —anette has risen with her things and begun walking toward the door.

"Dashanette I did not excuse you to go anywhere, especially to a place that may not exist."

"Ah, actually, Mr. Hort—" Hamster begins, but is interrupted.

"If you was a *real* teacher, you'd know the rules that say ain't no student can be kept from going to the school Wellness Center. It's the *law*. But you ain't no real teacher, you just a crusty ass, Star Trek-watchin', white-tennis-shoe-wearin', string cheese-eatin *sub!*"

Horton is dizzy; how the *hell* does she know that he eats string cheese?

"Dashanette!" Horton calls as she is struts out of sight.

"Mr. Horton," Hamster says. "Dashanette's right; *by law* all students must always be permitted to go to the Wellness Center."

"What? *Why?* What goes on there?"

"Well, it's confidential."

"Oh boy."

The class's refusal to participate in even the daintiest of academic tasks is balding Horton. He wasn't born yesterday— he knows that ninety percent of high school is utter bullshit, but goddamnit, *life* wasn't much different. Survival was all about bullshit. You take out the trash because if you don't, your house gets humid with the smell of old beer and ground chuck. You pay the cable bill on time because if you don't, you don't watch baseball. You substitute teach because if you don't, you don't eat string cheese. These are facts of life, and students either cope or get left behind. To be a good student does not require towering amounts of intellect, but simply a higher threshold for scholastic abuse. These kids had figured out that school was a waste of time; they just hadn't figured out that they had to suffer through it just the same.

"Ah, Dashanette. Poor girl, I hope she's not having one of her days," Hamster coos as the door closes behind her.

Horton moves on and asks Rolls Royce III if he'll read. There is no movement within his gargantuan sweater. Horton asks if Rolls Royce III is even *there*.

"Would you like to pass, Rolls Royce?" Hamster asks. "You *do* have the right to pass. If you would like to, you have to ask for permission. That's how it works. Ask to pass, and I will happily grant you a pass," says Hamster.

Rolls Royce III chooses not to vocally exercise his right to pass, but does continue passing inside his cotton warehouse. Horton walks over to Rolls Royce, but Hamster waves him off, whispering, "You know what I'd do? I'd just leave him alone right now. This might be one of his days."

Horton has naturally begun to wonder who, or what, this resident motivator motivates.

"Guys, we need someone to *read* a paragraph. That's it," Horton labors.

"Would anyone be *willing* to read one paragraph?" translates Hamster. "How about Sir Prize? Sir Prize, are you willing to read a paragraph?" he asks, joining Horton in this pathetic crusade of begging students to comply.

Sir Prize holds up a ruler decorated in sequins and peacock feathers.

"Ah, Sir Prize has decided to hold the safety stick today. I respect your choice to hold the safety stick, Sir Prize. You can be excused from the assignment."

"The *safety* stick?" Horton flails.

"The safety stick is used when someone isn't up for speaking, about anything," Hamster clarifies. "It's a way to give a student some space while assuring that he's still part of the community."

"The community?"

Horton is withering into the teacher's chair, shrinking and shrinking into the leather cushioning. He opens one of the drawers of the desk, counting on a flask being there.

"Master? Will you be willing to read just the first paragraph?" asks Hamster.

Following a dramatic sigh, Mah'Star grabs his worksheet and prepares to read. Horton's head has perked from the drawer. He looks at Mah'Star as if watching the hero in the movies that's about to clip the red wire and diffuse the bomb. Mah'Star inhales to read, all systems go! Work is about to manifest. Learning, school. Malcolm X, with his stern face of expectation, is looking down as the aim of his quote comes to fruition. "Education is our passport to the future, for tomorrow belongs to the people who prepare for it today."

Speak, Mah'Star, speak. Read. Learn. *Be.*

"Sexual harassment under California and Federal law is generally defined as—"

"Ma'Star already *been* suspended for two days for sexual harassment!" Yurheyenez yaps, looking at her nails.

"No!" Horton pleads.

"I ain't get suspended for that!" defends Mah'Star.

Horton grinds his teeth into baby powder.

"Your Highness, please don't speak about Master's affairs if they don't involve you," pampers Hamster.

"They do! He was harassin' *me!*"

"You a snitch! *And* you liked it! *And* I ain't even get suspended for that so *now* what, you moated-ass wrinkly whistleblowin' tuna-can-cootchie! You couldn't even be my number three!"

Prior to the interruption, for those two seconds, things were glorious. Horton's eyes closed and Mah'Star's words were the sound of rainfall on the porch after a drought, the sound of a broken-down car revving up. But now, the shining moment is buried under their regression into turbulence and laughter. Hamster supports all that is happening, stating that laughter is a natural response to stressful situations, like classwork.

Horton excuses himself for some fresh air. In a perfect world, *he'd* be the one checking into the Wellness Center, but as it turned out, life did not work that way. He was lucky there was another adult present, or he wouldn't even be authorized to leave for a much-needed break.

Moving through the halls, Horton feels trapped in a dream, the kind where he is being chased and no matter how fast he runs or how many times he outsmarts his pursuers, they are behind him, and when he finds someone whom he trusts, a comrade of some kind, he feels momentarily at ease and goes about escaping the nightmare until he learns that this comrade is against him and has been chasing him all along. Today is the nightmare, indeed, and Hamster is the comrade.

Earlier it was easy, practical even, to fault the students for the unproductiveness of the classroom; the kids were stubborn so any hiccups on the road to education were traceable to them. But Horton has seen enough now to know the root of this problem. Hamster was conditioning these kids to laugh in the face of responsibility.

They know that at any point they must be permitted to access the Wellness Center, where some freethinker in sandals is likely to tell them to chill on couches. If at any point they are denied their right to eat spicy Cheetos for breakfast, they know to feign malnourishment and unfitness to learn. Their right to freedom of speech can be called upon when an authoritarian attempts to censor their potty mouths, and when something doesn't sit right with them, the word *racism* is the quickest way to settle the issue in their favor. Saying "pass" is not only tolerated, but applauded, and finally, there is the trump card, the golden ticket to academic hibernation: the safety stick. Is it any surprise that these kids refuse to do work? Is it any, *Sir Prize?* Hell, back in high school Horton would have said "pass" till the cows came home had there been the option. He would have gotten so used to holding the safety stick that he'd have been able to draw it quicker than Wyatt Earp when called on in class. If he had been allowed to.

Horton has just returned from splashing water on his face.

"Hey look at *Horton*. Dude look like he found out the baby his!" remarks Abcd'n about Horton's miserable face.

"He look like he wearin' a thong for the first time!" chimes Yurheyenez.

"He look like he asked out an ugly bitch and got *shut down!*"

The kids celebrate another morning in which they have successfully avoided work. With the little time left in class, they authorize themselves to resume holocaustic computers games, reapply their headphones and begin to bob their heads to the music, bob with the volume up and their eyes closed. Everyone is flagrantly eating Cheetos. Yurheyenez seems to be simulating an audition for a raunchy burlesque show to the beat of nonexistent music. Horton has a demented, involuntary urge to both laugh and sob. His hands are shaking and there are sweat stains under his armpits the size of jellyfish.

Horton does not find these kids unintelligent or dreadful. His mental deterioration is not their doing. On the contrary, he has been delighted today by their creativity, especially as it related to verbal ridicule of peers and superiors. Their ability to somehow identify Horton's most pathetic human traits, without having ever met him, has been extraordinary. In a way, Horton wishes he could hang out with them as a peer, not a teacher, to enjoy them without having to beg them to do pointless work. In all the ways that cannot be quantified or proven, these kids possess qualities of brilliance, the kind of brilliance people go their whole lives struggling to have, the kind that is impossible to duplicate or imitate.

Watching them as the period winds down, Horton is reminded of third grade, which he hasn't thought of really since...third grade. Back then, a boy named Lawrence sat across from him. When the year started, Lawrence's hair was in braids, but they loosened over time without ever being rebraided or cut. When he came to school, his eyes were glazed and sleepless. He was, for the most part, quiet and stubborn for reasons Horton never understood. He said no when the teacher asked him to read. He sat with his arms folded when asked to do his math charts. When he refused to do work, the rest of the class quietly watched the way adults watch someone being arrested or rolled away in a stretcher: with curiosity and hints of unexplainable satisfaction.

One day, the class was writing a journal on what they wanted to be when they grew up. Lawrence was having trouble getting started. He was holding a gnawed stump of a pencil, tapping it on his desk. Horton was torn between writing about being a baseball player or the captain of a rogue pirate ship. He had his favorite pencil, a Teenage Mutant Ninja Turtles one. He'd been using it all year. It burst with juicy colors. He thought it helped him write better stories and do his math quicker.

As Horton decided what to write, his teacher asked him to

take the attendance to the office, as this was his daily task. When he returned, his journal book was there, but his pencil was not. Lawrence was looking at his notepad. Horton checked his pockets, checked the floor, looked inside his desk. It was gone. He looked at Lawrence again, who was writing in his journal for what may have been the first time that year.

Horton fidgeted. He began to feel hot inside and queasy.

"Horton? You need to write in your journal now, honey."

He looked up at his teacher and nodded, then looked back down at the table and then on the floor again. He looked in his desk.

"Horton, do you need a pencil? You need to get started," said the teacher again.

When he couldn't find his pencil, Horton's eyes filled with tears. He reached into his desk and pulled out an ordinary orange pencil with the red eraser. It had a smell of oldness, of detachment. Horton wiped his eyes and rubbed his nose. Horton's teacher walked next to him and lowered herself into a crouch.

"What's the matter?"

Horton began to cry.

"Something happened to my pencil."

Fortunately, the teacher knew of Horton's love for this pencil and was keen to the phenomenon of children being attached to seemingly arbitrary things.

"Oh dear," she said. "Well, where was it last?"

Horton explained that he'd left it on his desk when he took the attendance down to the office and when he returned it was gone. The teacher looked around the room, then at Lawrence, who was in a *rare* moment of uninterruptable devotion to academics. His concentration was immediately suspicious. She asked him if he'd seen the Ninja Turtles pencil, and based on

Lawrence's childish *un*mastery of lying, she seemed certain of who had the pencil. She attempted to give Lawrence the benefit of the doubt by asking him a series of questions like *Are you* sure *you haven't seen it?* and *Is it* possible *you accidentally picked it up thinking it was yours, just as an* accident?

Lawrence denied these insinuations. Quite softly, the teacher asked one more time if Lawrence had the pencil, and when he said he didn't have it, she decided to look in his desk for it. As she rose and began walking over, Lawrence reached into his desk, pulled out the Ninja Turtles pencil, and snapped it in half. Then he grabbed the dwarfed pencil *he'd* been using and threw it against the wall.

The teacher tried to restrain Lawrence but he wriggled free and picked up his chair and threw it across the room with ease. Then he collapsed and screamed into his jacket. He stuffed his jacket in his mouth and tore it, retching through clenched teeth, tears cascading down his face. Security arrived and picked him up. He began pulling his hair and punching his face and kicking whatever he could.

Horton forgot completely about his pencil and that it was now in pieces. Kids asked the teacher what was wrong with Lawrence, and she, rosy-cheeked and flustered, replied that he was having *one of his days*. Sometime later, the door opened and Lawrence was standing there, looking no different than he did every morning when he got to school, his eyes glossed over and his hair in ruins. He was escorted to his seat by his school mentor, a young man who typically took children in his office when they were having bad days. Lawrence sat down, and the mentor thanked him for sitting.

"Horton, you'll be happy to know that Lawrence has learned today that when he needs a pencil, he can ask for one instead of stealing someone else's."

Horton nodded.

"Can you tell Horton that you're sorry for taking his pencil?" asked the mentor to Lawrence, who said nothing. "Lawrence, can you please tell Horton you're sorry?"

After continued silence, the mentor answered for him: "Lawrence is very sorry."

The mentor then proceeded to reach into his pocket, pull out a colorful GI Joe led pencil, and award it to Lawrence.

"Now he's got his own pencil, so he won't have to take yours anymore, Horton. What do you have to say about that? Isn't that nice?" asked the mentor.

"Thanks," Horton said, an early experiment with sarcasm, as he was still clearly out a pencil himself.

The mentor, satisfied, left the room. Horton was writing with his orange stick of sawdust. Lawrence sat, analyzing his new pencil, thinking about something. He did not seem to be preparing to do any classwork, and the teacher knew that with the day he was having, she better not push him. After a while, Lawrence reached across the table and placed the pencil in front of Horton, who looked up, looked into Lawrence's eyes, which were soggy from raw emotion. Lawrence seemed to be bottling in hatred, but not toward Horton or their teacher or class, but toward something else altogether, something much bigger, much harder to explain.

"I'll trade you," Lawrence said, looking at Horton's pencil.

Sadly, the mentor was not there to witness this development, or take credit for it. Horton accepted Lawrence's offering, and that was the end of it. Lawrence continued to have issues that year, and did not return to the school the next year for fourth grade. No one ever found out where he ended up, or saw him again.

Now Horton watches his students blow off their final minutes of class. He watches Abcd'n and Sir Prize bob their heads to their music, while Yurheyenez cocks and rotates her hips in a comical and depressingly skillful striptease impersonation. He thinks of Lawrence and those eyes of frustration and longing, and how he suffered nearly every day with some similar incident. He imagines his students today as third graders, enduring similar issues, finding it difficult to follow rules, make friends, and make sensible decisions. He looks at Hamster.

"There should be no such thing as a safety stick," Horton whispers to Hamster, startling him. "Their prescription of school-sanctioned copouts is weak. It's selling them short."

"You're entitled to your opinion," replies Hamster, a kumbay-ya counter. "The safety stick comes from years of research and discourse. The whole country is implementing it into their pedagogy."

"Oh Jesus."

Horton can't believe all the fake words he's just heard.

Yes, alternate approaches to teaching *are* necessary, Horton agrees. Of course traditional expectations are null and void to any kids from tough neighborhoods and broken homes. The *pedagogy* behind the safety stick can be backed by positive results, and Horton does not doubt this, for it is reasonable and considerate to *implement* circumstantial systems that ease the daily life of disadvantaged kids. *In theory*. But all the research that goes into *implementing* this *pedagogy,* all these tried and true safety sticks and wellness centers, are futile when placed in the hands of someone like Hamster.

Hamster was a bitch, the type to get overcharged at the taqueria and wear it, the type to get his parking spot stolen without throwing up the bird in retaliation, the kind who thinks he is helping people by being nice, when really, he is screwing everyone. Hamster didn't listen to the music these kids listened to, he'd probably never recognized the beat in any musical composition. He probably listened to U2 or Train, and a man in his position could not afford to be a fan of such music. He could not relate to his students or contribute much besides a smile and a soft request for them to stay on task. He was not a product of the same city, not a product of public schools. They'd named him Hamster, and he allowed it. How was that for fucking *pedagogy*?

Horton, of course, was not the adolescent guru. Rarely did he leave a school feeling respected by students. That day was no exception. But as the class empties, he can't help but think of Lawrence, and what he might be doing now. His students bob away, insulated by their headphones, and he wants to go out and stop them, and bring them back, tell them about Lawrence. More than anything, Horton hopes to wake up the next day to a phone call offering him the tactfully evasive job of high...school...classroom...teacher. Oddly, he wouldn't mind returning, if only to be insulted by them some more.

"Day Off"

Horton is startled awake at 5:09 a.m. by an automated phone call telling him his job that day has been cancelled. Just like that, he is out one hundred and sixty dollars. He looks out his window. It is still dark. There are periodic whishing noises of cars going by—the sounds of people whose days have already begun. Ordinarily, Horton would sympathize with them for having to wake up so early, but today, he envies them for having jobs. The soft noises begin to lullaby him back to sleep, that is, until he is startled by another call from the district. He answers hoping it is a new job, but the robotic voice has different news. It proceeds to remind him that his job has been cancelled.

To hear about a cancellation, please press one . . .

Horton hangs up. In the next fifteen minutes, he receives three more calls—with just enough time in between to wake him as he falls back asleep—reminding him that he no longer has a job. This happened sometimes: repeated reminders, a glitch in the substitute database system. It really pissed him off. Actually, it really pissed everyone off. Horton remembers when, a couple of years ago at the annual substitute convention, a collection of disgruntled subs expressed their views on the job distribution system.

"I don't care how you do it, just stop waking me up with

those calls!" one garbled.

"And if my job gets cancelled, why the hell do I need to hear about it fifteen times?" said another.

"Yeah! At *five* in the morning!"

"I got high blood pressure!" another wheezed. "One of these goddamned calls is going to kill me!"

So the district developed a new system, an online database on which substitutes could manage their workload and assign themselves jobs. It was immediately deemed unacceptable by substitutes, who were disgusted that the Internet was now a prerequisite for success in their line of work; many subs did not have Internet, or computers.

"You're telling us that the little money we make needs to be spent on things we can't stand, or afford?" they lobbied, unionizing, as it were. "Just because it's easy for some doesn't mean it's easy for all! I get along just *fine* without Internet."

"You know what this is? *Extortion!*"

Meanwhile, as some substitutes threatened to strike, other substitutes *with* Internet logged on and horded all of the available jobs. It got ugly, and eventually both the phone systems and online systems were reinstated and adjusted: jobs could no longer be horded, and phone calls were allegedly barred from coming in any earlier than six, or incessantly. That day, however, it was clear that the latter of their claimed improvements had not actually been fulfilled.

Horton falls back asleep and is awoken midmorning by an unceremonious noise outside. By now, it is light out. Horton plods to the window and looks out to find a street protest. There are signs and chants of distress and demands for change. Horton sees from the signs that this protest has been organized against mimes—and all forms of mimery—for their discrimination against mute persons, and boy scouts, though at the moment, it is unclear as to how mimes offend boy scouts.

STOP THIS CRIME

NO MORE MIMES

FOR SCOUTS AND MUTES ALIKE

IT'S TIME!

The chant is reinforced by faces of inner struggle, being theatrically (and ironically) mimed. The protest shifts into the middle of the street, where cars are trying to get to work. The cars are forced into gridlock. Horton wants to open his window, lean out and yell, "If mutes could talk they'd tell you all to get a job!" That would show them. Then he looks down, realizes it is midmorning, and that he is still in his pajamas. He, too, has no job, and therein lies a problem.

When Horton doesn't have a job, he feels unauthorized to judge people who he wants to judge. He is essentially left to his thoughts, worrying he has made a wrong decision to be a sub. He fears his mind is being wasted, that he has taken the lazy way out while everyone else is rewarded for hard work. He feels no better than the kids who live at home until they're thirty, the adults that collect unemployment and sit on the computer, the people currently outside his window.

Initially, Horton justified his job by thinking of it only as a bill payer while he concentrated on poetry. In his free time, and even while subbing, he wrote and edited poems in hopes that his persistence would yield him the profession he pursued. He had always heard about how comedians worked at Arby's and lived out of their cars before catching their big break, or how musicians worked graveyard shifts at anchovy canneries before writing that chart-topping single. Comparatively, Horton was fine with substitute teaching while he refined his art, but that was years ago. To that day, he had still only ever published one poem, and that was in high school. He found he wasn't writing as much as he once did. When he sat down with a pen and pad, he had a difficult time starting—he couldn't seem to get past the fact that no matter what he wrote and rewrote, no matter how polished and poignant he thought his work was, there was a good chance it would go unpublished. This induced writer's block. In fact, he couldn't even claim to have writer's block because he could not claim to be a writer.

There are holes in Horton's socks and the kitchen floor is sticky and freezing, the way linoleum is in San Francisco no matter the month. He opens his fridge and mourns the emptiness. There is a Tupperware container, which once held a potato, but is now empty. There is also soy sauce, and in the way back there are some maraschino cherries that have barges of mold treading through the red syrupy seas. He is about to rally his spare change for a trip to the corner store when his phone rings. It is the automated substitute system, as recognized by his caller ID. Horton is furious, certain that he is being told again that he has no job. But this time, it's a job.

It's across town, but that doesn't matter. In the event that a job is assigned after the school day has started, by law, the substitute is allotted an hour and a half—this being the time assumed it takes a geriatric woman to navigate buses across the city—to arrive. Horton has a car, so he can take his time. For the moment, he is not distracted by self-disappointment. He no longer questions the direction of his life, because at least his *present* direction is toward one hundred and sixty dollars. On the way to work, he passes all of the protestors and laughs. No one is listening to them. No one cares.

His commute leads him out of the fog and into the sun, symbolizing today's change in fortune. On the street where he parks, Hispanic men are pushing Popsicle carts. Horton has a few minutes to kill, so he buys a coconut Popsicle and works up a sweat eating it. How the day has turned around.

The double-doors to the school are made of heavy wood, a clear indication that the building is old, perhaps pre-World War II. Once inside, Horton takes his jacket off to prevent the sweat stains under his armpits from widening. The hallways smell of rusted metal and cafeteria food. In the main office where Horton tries to check in, he is asked to sit while the secretary searches for his assignment. The woman appears to be inconvenienced by Horton. She smells like someone who was caught in a hailstorm of perfume bottles.

"Are you sure you're supposed to be here?" she asks, without seeming interested in an answer.

"The job came in late this morning, if that helps."

"No."

Horton nods.

"Why would that help?" she belabors, then rolls her eyes. "I found it."

"What room shall I go to?" Horton asks.

"You're not here."

"Huh?"

"The teacher you're in for no longer works here. He switched schools over the summer. Looks like they didn't update the system."

Horton, at this point, has confirmed that the school's heater is on. There is hot air blowing from the wall vents despite the weather outside, which is causing the inside of the many-windowed school to roast like a green house. A drop of sweat has just fled his armpit for a very slimy and irritating joyride down his hip.

"So I have to go to a different school?" he asks.

The secretary simply stares at Horton, an it-would-appear-that-way-now-wouldn't-it kind of stare.

"You guys got the heater on or something?" Horton asks.

"Don't know."

"Is it not hotter than hell in here?"

"You'd best be on your way, wouldn't you say? There is a class of students that needs you to be concerned with their education right now over the current state of school ventilation."

"Where is your bathroom?" Horton snorts.

"Down the hall, to the left."

Horton leaves the scented, unenchanting woman and pays a visit to the water fountain to cool down. The water fountain has nothing aquatic to say, just a few gags of rusty dribble, which Horton concludes would leave him further dehydrated if suckled. Everything in this school is working oppositely. His sweating is now torrential.

Horton enters the faculty lounge where he was told the bathroom was. There is a dining table surrounded by seats. There are some cupboards and a small kitchen sink. There are cutting boards, knives, plates, and forks. Next to this is a microwave, then a refrigerator. The implication is that the teachers prepare and eat their lunches in this small quarter daily. Directly next to all of this is a toilet. With a door that does not appear to be noise proof. As Horton relieves himself, he envisions the inevitable moments at lunch when one teacher is introducing ingredients to his body while another is riotously bidding them adieu next to him.

He leaves for his car, where he hears the faint cries of something familiar. He pauses and concentrates. The noises are coming from down the street, getting louder and louder as he waits.

STOP THIS CRIME

NO MORE MIMES

FOR SCOUTS AND MUTES ALIKE
IT'S TIME!

They've managed to protest their way across the city. Unemployment must be energizing, he thinks, then shudders, admitting the similarities of his job to unemployment; it is approaching eleven and he has not yet worked a minute.

STOP THIS CRIME
NO MORE MIMES
FOR SCOUTS AND MUTES ALIKE
IT'S TIME!

They stampede for change and Horton slams the door to get away. He rushes over Twin Peaks, the large mountain that separates the east from the west side of the city, essentially barricading the fog into the west. Within minutes he has rolled up his windows and turned on his wipers to deflect the heavyset fog of the west. People are walking with umbrellas, whereas virtually seconds ago, people were fanning themselves.

Once parked at the next school, he exits his car and is blindsided by curtains of snarling mist. The parts of his shirt where sweat had accumulated are now sticking to him, freezing to him.

He pries open the door to the school, another heavy wooden door, and it slams behind him as loud as Paul Bunyan demanding order in the court. Horton hopes that the secretary in this office will have a little more human sensibility than the last one.

"That's some weather out there," Horton says to the secretary as he enters the main office.

"You must be the substitute," she deduces.

"I am. Just came from the other side of the city. San Francisco Unified is giving me the grand tour today."

"Won't be the last."

"Amen."

Horton is shivering. The dewdrops on his arm have inspired goosebumps. The office is as cold as outside, or quite possibly colder. There seems to be a consistent draft shooting under his shirt from somewhere, perhaps the wall vents. This gives Horton an odd suspicion.

"Say, I know this sounds stupid, but the air conditioner isn't on, is it?"

"Here at Jerry Garcia Elementary, you learn to bundle up."

"It's damn near fifty degrees outside!" Horton cries. "Rain is literally suspended in the air!"

"Yes."

"Schools on the other side of the city are trying to simulate the inside of a kiln!"

"You learn to wear a scarf in these parts."

"You have no control of your central air?"

"It ain't all that bad so long as you wear some long johns."

Horton is now trembling. How will he survive a day in this? He already feels ill and it's been less than five minutes. How do kids *do* this? It was a modern-day form of coalmines. There needed to be some proposition that banned children from having to learn in both arctic and broiling conditions such as these. Public schools, while free, should still *function*!

To Horton, this all seems like an easy fix. Perhaps the engineer controlling the central heat of these schools can be told that, as a rule of thumb, the east side of the city is sunny, and the west side is not. San Francisco has no seasons. The summer is not warm, in the winter it doesn't snow, the fall yields no colors. Everything is year-round fog on the west and sun on the east. That's essentially all there is to it.

"So, it appears as though you've been double assigned today," the secretary says finally. "You were called to fill in a position that already has a sub covering for it."

"Naturally."

Horton has heard of this happening, but has never experienced it himself. How—once an assignment is officially accepted by one person—does it then continue to be offered?

"Now, there is something you might be able to do to get a job today," the secretary says. "The substitute that picked up the job might have *wanted* the day off in the first place. She might have picked it up only because they really needed a sub. You never know. You might want to offer to take her job for her. Who doesn't want a day off, after all?"

Substitutes, Horton thinks, *that's* who. They don't like days off because they don't get paid.

"So, if you want my advice," she continues, "you might want to go to her classroom and offer to take over for her today. You know, offer her a day off."

"You mean offer to take her money?" Horton asks.

"I hadn't thought of it like that. Well, it's room one thirteen if you want to give it a shot," she says, adjusting her scarf, blowing warm air into her hands, and rubbing them together.

Horton leaves the office toward the classroom. The door slams behind him and echoes hollowly. The school has the feeling of a haunted meat locker. Horton strategizes the best—or most flowery—way of presenting this substitute the opportunity to lose money to him.

The door of the classroom indicates this is a second grade class. He peers inside and sees kids at little desks, sitting in little seats, reading. There is a colorful rug in the corner of the room and a big cushioned seat where the teacher likely tells stories. Suspended high on the wall and orbiting the room is the alphabet and pictures of animals that begin with the corresponding letter. There are cupboards of crayons and poster boards for art projects, and there is a small zone with a few computers likely for children to share during free time.

Horton knocks on the door, steps inside the room, sees the substitute with whom he is about to negotiate, and immediately regrets his decision. Horton has crossed paths with this woman before and she was no easier to deal with than ancient Chinese torture methods. She was like a terrible itch on the bottom of your foot with a cast on, or trying to write a very opinionated and incensed letter with a pen that is running out of ink. She was Randi.

"I'm Randi. I'm a substitute," she announces.

Immediately, she is in front of Horton.

"Sssssssssss, everyone working. Ssssssssss, reading quietly pleasssSSsssssSSSsse," she directs her students.

"Hi," she reiterates.

"Hi, I'm Horton."

"I'm not the usual teacher. I'm just a substitute."

"I'm also a substitute. We worked together once in the computer lab. At Monroe Middle School. I'm not sure if you remember."

"Are you here to help out today?"

"Um, in a way. Actually, that's what I'm trying to get to the bottom of."

"Sssssssssss, reading ssssSSSSsssSSSsSsSilently," she addresses her students. "Pleasssse, everyone. Children, SilensssSSSSe."

Not a single child is making a peep or doing anything that warrant*sSs* such persi*ssSsss*tant sssSssummons for ssSSSsedated behavior.

"I'm a substitute. I could really use your assistance in the class today. I've got the young ones."

"That's kind of why I'm here," Horton advertises. "You see, we were double booked today. I also got a call for this job late this morning and accepted it. So it seems there are two teachers for one job."

Unsurprisingly, Randi is confused.

"So they've got two of us today for this job? Oh god, is the class that bad? They probably dished us a slew of criminals!" She looks around. "I knew it," she says.

The second graders are quietly reading.

"They didn't assign two people to teach one job," Horton attempts, "they mistakenly assigned one job to two people."

This even confuses Horton.

"So you've come to help out? I could really use your assistance."

"If you don't want to work today, I can stay and you can have the day off, if you'd like. I'm perfectly fine staying here. You can take the day off."

"Oh, I could never. SssssssssSssSssss. I have so many billsssss."

Horton feels the time to leave is now. Everything from this point forward will waste his time. It was no use with this woman. He needed to cut his losses and make a move. He takes one step to the door. She reacts with one step closer to him.

"I can't ever take days off, you see. My son's piano lessons are sixty bucks a pop. Sixty *bucks*. Just to learn 'Hot Cross Buns!' Can you believe it?"

Horton takes a step back, which is matched again.

"I've got to take all the work I can. Work is never guaranteed, and the crooks don't even pay our health care. Are you *kidding* me? I've got a big old swollen vein somewhere on the back of my knee, so I have to sleep on my side, which is really uncomfortable. I can't sleep at all. I see a hypnotist for that. It doesn't help. I keep going. And all of those doctor bills add up, and I have to pay for them out of my pocket. You gotta be *kidding*."

Horton looks at the door, wishing Randi was kidding. Randi hisses. She will not let him free.

"I just got my jury duty notice in the mail. I'm thinking, are you *kidding?*"

She stares at Horton, daring him to move.

"Produce is so overpriced right now. Two dollars for a stinking avocado. How do I *afford* this?"

Horton looks at the second graders for salvation.

"Don't even get me started on my ex-husband."

Horton gasps. "So you're staying today?"

"Ssssssssss…"

Horton starts walking away.

"I could *really* use the assistance."

Randi slithers after Horton.

"I'm *freezing* right now!" she cries.

Yet another door in the school slams shut, trapping Randi in her igloo. Horton jogs through the cold marble hallway toward the exit. It is now almost noon. He has driven across the city and associated with a series of excruciating souls on a fruitless odyssey for work. Everyone had work that day, everyone would make money but Horton, it seemed; all *he* has achieved is a lower gas tank, a worn outlook on mankind, and a Popsicle. Horton is having a "day off."

Getting to his car, he hears a noise. A rhythm of some kind. A chant. Horton can see nothing through the fog. The marching and chanting gets louder, Horton feels threatened. He has no idea what direction the chants are coming from. He only knows they are getting louder, and a little clearer. As he stands at his car, frozen, the sounds intensify. The steps are clearer, the words of the chant decipherable, louder.

STOP THIS CRIME

NO MORE MIMES

FOR SCOUTS AND MUTES ALIKE
IT'S TIME!

The reigning hymn of unemployment is yet to be extinguished!

Now they are upon Horton.

"IF MUTES COULD TALK THEY'D SAY GET A JOB!" hollers Horton, but this counter-protest is drowned out and unheard. Horton is circled by them. They rub their eyes of fake tears, mangling their mouths into steep-parabola frowns. They orbit with hypnotizing slowness. It is as though they are not decrying all things mime, but stalking Horton, sniffing out weak prey, zeroing in on a potential recruit for their movement. After all, who wanders residential streets in the middle of a weekday besides a fellow unemployed simpleton? They sense he is kin. The kin of unemployment, the kin of hey-what-are-you-up-to-tomorrow? . . . NOTHING.

They continue their stupefying rounds and persist with chants for change, for awareness, for progression. After all, what better do they have to do? The mimes begin to motion with their fingers for Horton to join in the movement. Their midday parade for justice would be stronger with another comrade. They figure that he, like them, has nothing better to do.

Banana Pancakes

High School Chemistry . . . and Beyond

By the time Horton learns he is an Internet sensation, it will be too late. While he snores from a night of binge drinking, his YouTube video, which he does not know exists, thrives like cancer cells at a microwave expo. Nothing can undo a career like YouTube, and Horton is about to endure this truth in its most unforgiving form.

Horton is hung over because it is March 18, meaning the previous night was March 17, and he is Irish. His memory of last night is murky. No breath, no matter how deep, seems to bring him oxygen. He feels like he ate plates of rusty hubcaps. He doesn't usually get that drunk, not even on St. Patty's Day. Perhaps all of his tribulations that year, like infrequent work, scarce sexual encounters, unpardonable colleagues, and journals of unpublished poetry caught up to him last night in the melee and playful spirit of his Irish heritage.

At work, sitting on the bathroom floor, Horton finds that the coolness of the tiles is a refreshing combatant to the putrid inferno of a St. Patrick's Day hangover. His phone will play a pivotal role, he feels, in filling in the blanks from last night, so as he clings to the toilet bowl, he pulls it out and reads his texts, hoping for answers.

See you in twenty. Did you eat yet?
8:33 p.m.
You gonna drink green beer?
8:37 p.m.

Horton remembers responding "no," to that text, because he sees no point in green beer, and if his memory serves him correctly, he didn't drink any. The thought of beer, however, inspires Horton to uncork a dam of puke, which is primarily green. So there goes that. The vomit also fizzes black, reminding Horton of the concoctions that kids and fat people make at soda fountains when they inject every flavor into their cup and pretend it tastes good when it really tastes like caramel and Lysol. These observations lead to sustained vomiting.

Where did you go? We're at McTeague's on Polk.
9:44 p.m.

Horton deduces that he was separated from his group at some point. Snapshots of his memory show him stumbling up and down Polk Street, hocking loogies and bumping into crowds of drunkards with leprechaun hats. Parking meters, parked cars, light poles—Horton semi-recalls wrestling these objects. And losing.

I'm worried about you.
11:02 p.m.

Horton's reply, according to his outbox, is *Ijgs nkot injside?,* which evidently led his friends to give up on him, as there are no follow-up texts for a while. Horton was on his own.

He embraces the toilet, takes an unfulfilling breath. He is still excessively drunk, which is a great way to lose his job. Luckily, he has no class first period, which enables him to wallow on the men's bathroom floor as he pieces his night together with cellular clues. In that habitat of assorted pubic hair and ancient wads of filth, Horton scrolls through his outbox, which has substantially less traffic than his inbox, indicating he was either very busy or in a state of mental debilitation. Or both. He falls asleep for an unknown amount of time, nestled against the porcelain. He is awaken when the bell rings, telling him it's time to shape up and get to class. But before he stands, he discovers a peculiar text from later last night.

HAHA, banana pancakes! BANANA PANCAKES! Classic, bro.
1:13 a.m.

Banana pancakes, he wonders, but can do nothing about it for the time being. He splashes water over his face and heads to his class, twelfth grade chemistry. This is a questionable circumstance considering Horton *failed* chemistry in high school and is by no means classified to teach any form of science.

A herd of students laugh at Horton in the hallways. Their taunting makes him worry that his hangover is as disastrous publicly as it is internally. Then *another* group of students crow amusedly at his sight, which causes him to adjust his hair and quicken his steps to the classroom. He enters, slams the door behind him, and wipes his brow as if he has just escaped the persistent murderer in a horror saga. But everyone knows they always come back.

Horton's students are irrationally giddy. They have their phones out and seem to have no intention of holstering them anywhere but in front of their faces. Over the years, Horton has noted the rising epidemic of electronics in schools; even elementary school kids have phones now and feel it is their right to play with them in class. Parents fight to uphold their toddlers' rights to bear electronics because, *What if there is a disaster? A terrorist attack, earthquake, or escaped child molester?* Being that the district cannot overlook such appalling hypotheticals, babies are permitted to picture message each other and chat with their little thumbs in a classroom where learning is expected, and when percentiles plummet on standardized tests, those same parents raise hell, demanding better learning conditions. By the time these kids are in high school, their obsession with electronics morphs into outright dependency, and they fall down stairs and drive into fire hydrants because at every moment, their eyes are fastened to the machines in their hands.

Today, Horton's students are somehow more drawn than usual to their phones.

"All right, all right, boys and girls. You're juniors and seniors, you know the drill," Horton grumbles. "Let's act like adults."

He limps over to the classroom bell, the same bell at the counter of hotels or car rentals, and dings it once. About two kids perk up. He dings it again but it is worthless; such a noise only works with dogs at dinnertime. Horton then picks up the Classroom Log of Peace, which is a rain stick, and gives that a try. He turns it upside down, and the soothing clicks of the Peruvian instrument, which are meant to induce children into an intoxicating trance of discipline, are offensively ignored.

"If you'll just put your phones away and direct your attention to the board, we shouldn't have any problems today. For those of you who don't know me from other classes, my name is—"

"BANANA PANCAKES!" a kid blurts, postponing Horton.

Never in his life has he heard the phrase "banana pancakes" twice in one day.

"I'm sorry?"

No one responds. But some kids are on the verge of atomic laughter.

"Banana pancakes?"

The kids spurt pent-up cackles like manholes shooting from sewer systems.

"Right, well as I was saying, you can call me Mr. Hagardy," says Horton. "Your teacher has left me a packet for you to complete, some busy work. I'll write the reference pages on the board and let you guys be on your way. Oh, and I'll be *collecting* this work," he threatens, virtually the only leverage he has over his students.

When Horton turns his back to the class, he hears the words *banana pancakes* tribally retched by nearly half the class, as if banana pancakes are the school's mascot and this is the state football championship.

"What the *fuck*," Horton hisses to himself, bewildered, HUNGOVER.

The kids whisper among themselves. Through the laughter, Horton hears the static of a low quality speaker, like that of a phone, begin to blare.

"Phones away, please," Horton dribbles.

"But it's banana pancakes," a student reports.

"Phones *away* please," Horton repeats.

BANANA *FUCKING* PANCAKES. OH HEAVENS! BANANA PANCAKES FOR YOUR DELICATE SOUL! DO NOT DENY ME OR YOURSELF LAYERS OF GRIMY FULFILLMENT!

Horton freezes. He has not just heard a student, and he knows this for three reasons. First, the voice carries the raspy hollowness of a cell phone speaker. Second, no one has spoken with such verbiage since 1750 England.

And finally—the voice sounds strikingly similar to his own.

The student pauses the video, mid . . . whatever it is.

Kids are staring at Horton. Laughter is scarcely being restrained. Classroom order is unstable. Horton's hangover is lethal.

"Wha—what'cha guys got over there?" he peeps, almost certain now that the voice he just heard slurring the nonsensical

Shakespearean plea is somehow his.

"Banana pancakes," responds a kid.

Horton sighs.

"What is banana pancakes?"

"It's you, Mr. Hagardy. Remember?"

A student rises to bring the phone over to Mr. Hagardy.

"Here. Take a look. At yourself."

The kid starts the video by touching the screen. Horton sees that the video has already been viewed 24,789 times, and was posted less than twelve hours ago. This fact accelerates Horton's heart in a very abnormal and sickly manner. Then he watches the video called "Banana Pancakes."

It is St. Patrick's Day night, last night—Horton deduces this by the crowd of green and the drunken banter. Horton sees himself sitting on the curb cross-legged with his hands folded in his lap, swaying like a sleeping fish beneath a hurricane. The large crowd surrounding Horton suggests he has been there a while; he's *earned* the crowd. Grunts and other noises of insanity are emitted by him. Saliva sprays with each exhalation.

"What are you going to do for her?" asks an unidentified teenager, the one shooting the film with his phone.

"Cook banana pancakes!" Horton gargles on the curb. "How many times I gotta . . . I cook anything, every day for that ass. I'm a real man, you know how that goes. You know."

Girls giggle in the background. A fat cop is enjoying this in the periphery, ignoring his job and the fact that San Francisco's Irish youth often interpret St. Patty's Day as a time to test their brawling skills on the city's most harmless bumpkins.

"Is that Mr. Hagardy?" a random teenager asks. The response is affirming, and loud. "Hey, that dude subs at my school. Wow, *look* at him!"

"Fuck yeah I *teach*!" Horton slurs. "You don't know a thing about cooking. Get me a beer."

"You sure?" asks the high school student, who himself is drinking a beer, this also being a situation that the cop does not address.

"Where's the *girl?*" Horton demands.

"I'm right here."

A woman with wide anatomy lumbers into the frame. Her blonde hair is shorter than her shoulders, her shirt does not confine her abdomen. It also leaves her chest dramatically exposed, a feature that catches every man's eye on St. Patty's Day. Especially Horton's. Though her breasts have grown triangularly toward her armpits, they *are* large. Her presentation is loose and beefy—enough to pass as Rubenesque, but certainly not voluptuous.

"My voluptuous, dew-kissed clover," drools Horton in his finest romantic tongue, "come hither so that I may plunder and devour your ass."

Horton, judging by his face, has no idea what he's just said. The crowd gasps in appreciation. The girl, drunk herself, is trying to appear offended, though hints of interest squirt from her green-glittered eyes. Horton continues to sway, hock loogies on himself, and threaten the cameraman, who is one of his students.

Since St. Patrick's Day is one of those days when all ages celebrate openly in the street until late, Horton has unfortunately been discovered in a ghastly state by some high school students who have decided to stay out way past curfew. Now there is a substantial crowd around Horton's monologue, consisting of the whale he is vehemently courting, a merry cop, some of Horton's own friends, and a gang of adolescents who are being given the power to end Horton's career with one click of a button. And since there is *nothing* more exciting to a high school student than poorly videotaping something and posting it to YouTube, Horton's odds are stacked against him.

"Get the camera away, you faggot!" Horton cries, a poor career move, especially in San Francisco. The adolescent shoves the camera further into Horton's face, capturing frothy noodles of drool looping from his mouth. Horton loses interest in the camera.

"And what are you going to do for her?" asks a student.

"Stop egging him on! You guys are mean!" pipes the large woman, Horton's goal.

"BANANA PANCAKES!" Horton lashes. "THAT'S WHAT I'M ABOUT TONIGHT. GETTING REAL FEISTY WITH THAT EXTRA PREGNANT DOSE OF CHOWDER!" he bellows, pointing at the woman. Then he announces each ingredient of banana pancakes and states that he will "weld them sensually." All she must do in return is donate to him her "buoyant dimensions," with which he will realistically accomplish a frustrating amount of nothing.

"Will you make me anything I want, darling?" she blubbers.

"Anything," slobbers Horton. "Banana pancakes, though. That's the one tonight."

"Will you make me corned beef and potatoes? Moist and soft?" She bats her green eyelashes.

It takes Horton a moment to process this request, and when he does, his eyes gape and tremor madly.

"CORN BEEF POTATOES!?" he wails, staring blankly into the ground. "DO YOU WANT...NOT THE FONDLING?

"ARE YOUR PORTIONS NOT GENEROUS ENOUGH... ALREADY? BUT REALLY, I LOVE THE REALM YOU'RE GETTING COZY WITH, REAL NAUGHTY CUSHIONY HANDFULS."

Now it is the woman's turn to process what Horton has just

said, but that doesn't take long, and the result is not in Horton's favor.

The fun and games are promptly over—no woman, no matter how drunk, can stand being told she is fat, and so Horton has just lost his hungry prospect to his romantic tongue. She flops away.

"Wait. What I *do*?!" he bellows. "WHAT?!" He is jolting his head, ill with infatuation.

"You called her fat, Mr. Hagardy. She's gone," answers the student.

Horton eyes the student skeptically, then hatefully, then dreadfully.

"NO!"

He tries to rise but scrapes his knee and falls before he ever lifts off, breaking the fall with his elbows. It's ugly.

"I was going to make banana pancakes! For the FUCKING MORNING TIME!" he cries from his knees.

"She's gone, forever."

"You're an *infant*," retorts Horton. At this point he commences to rolling around on the sidewalk like a desert animal in cool soil. The cop decides to tell him he will have to go home now. Horton is not listening.

"BANANA *FUCKING* PANCAKES. OH HEAVENS! BANANA PANCAKES FOR YOUR DELICATE SOUL! DO NOT DENY ME OR YOURSELF LAYERS OF GRIMY FULFILLMENT!" sobs Horton.

People are wondering out loud about what exactly Horton is referring to—pancakes or bulbous fornication.

"Banana pancakes," Horton gasps, pounding the cement desperately.

"Dude, turn it off, this isn't even funny anymore," a kid says.

"Yeah, hey, I think Mr. Hagardy's life is over," the

cameraman assumes, not making the connection that the only way Mr. Hagardy's life will end is if *he* decides to publish the slander.

In the classroom, Horton nearly faints when the video ends. Just in the last two minutes, Horton sees it's been viewed a thousand more times. He realizes that he's done something very bad. He's made one of those mistakes everyone makes at least once, one of those things that happens at least once a week in every bar in America. It just so happens that Horton's blunder was witnessed, recorded, and distributed like fliers from a chopper. He does not ask who posted it, he does not wonder why his friends didn't stop him or drag him away before it got ugly, or at the very least take that stupid little phone and smash it to pieces in the kid's face—it is too late for all of that. Horton excuses himself to the toilet where he hoses down the wall with an emerald stream of bile.

Horton pulls out his phone and reads the text again.

HAHA, banana pancakes! BANANA PANCAKES! Classic, bro.

After prolonged regurgitation, Horton goes to the principal and is immediately sent home, for his face shows the pale emptiness of a man infected with a virus that can end a school's population.

Horton spends the rest of the day in bed. When he gets up, he microwaves a pizza and warily opens the Internet browser to check the statuses of some things. YouTube is attended. He stares at the white search bar, then types "ban" and the site immediately assumes he is looking for a video called "banana pancakes." With sadness, Horton follows the suggestion and is led to a video that now has over one hundred thousand hits. Comments on the video are flying in as recent as "two seconds ago." He hits refresh, and the views increase by seventy-eight.

"Jesus."

Then Horton goes to the district's substitute database online to see where he is assigned tomorrow, hoping it is an elementary school; younger kids are less likely to have seen his cinematic debut. Horton discovers his substitute assignments are being canceled as rapidly as "banana pancakes" is gaining fame. The next two months of work have already been wiped clean. When he navigates through the database and tries to reassign himself those jobs in hopes that there has been a glitch, the jobs are immediately re-cancelled before his eyes.

More or less, Horton has been fired. Everyone has seen Banana Pancakes. The snippet has ruined him. Technology has ruined him. Once upon a time, Horton was amused by the annihilation of careers as a result of misused technology, like midlife-crisis-plagued politicians who accidentally published nudie shots of their flub and balls on public forums. These were adults making utter fools of themselves due to an inability to act their age, and operate modern technology. This was purely rich! But *he's* the fool this time. Thousands of people have watched him, been entertained by him, been appalled by him, and ensured that he will be unemployed and disgraced by his family, just as his Uncle Hogan was months before when he put out a status on Facebook *during* a heart attack. Horton has outdone his uncle! *He* is the disgrace.

Throughout his career, the insignificance of his job always upset him. No longer is that the case. In the most twisted and ironic way, his dream has come true. He is now unforgettable, and yet he'd give everything he had, which was very little, to be back in the classroom as the ghostly unmemorable shrew that is the substitute teacher.

It turned out the kid was correct at the end of the video when he said, "Hey, I think Mr. Hagardy's life is *over*."

* * *

Months go by.

Horton has a beard and he wears flannel and doesn't put on shoes when he walks to the corner store. He stinks. Horton stops looking on YouTube to rue the success of his video; last he checked it was at two million hits. The video still flourishes, however, and Horton knows this because of the praise he receives when people recognize him on the streets.

"Grimy intense fulfillment!" people yell playfully; Horton flips them off.

"Do you want . . . *not* fondling?" he hears when he rides the bus. Horton frequently gets off the bus at . . . *not* his stop . . . to elude harassment from his fans.

Thousands of reenactments, remixes, songs and video blogs have been posted in dedication to the man behind "Banana Pancakes." The video has appeared on popular comedy websites and TV shows like *Ebaumsworld*, *CollegeHumor*, *The Onion*, and *Tosh.0*. Sometimes, Horton sees people wearing shirts of him sitting like a sloshed Buddhist on the curb, screaming into the night, with a dialog bubble coming out of him that says "BANANA PANCAKES!"

Horton wishes people had lives of their own. Then he might still have *his* life.

* * *

One night, in about his fifth month of unemployment—after drinking from a bottle of cheap rum, which he does some nights to indulge his childhood aspiration to be a pirate—Horton looks at YouTube. 54,345,128 views; he weeps. He is not a pirate. He is not even a substitute teacher. He will never have another job—YouTube provides the most worthless, destructive fame possible. Horton falls asleep that night against a pillowcase soggy with tears, next to honey-roasted peanuts wrappers, in a house that smells like skid-marked boxers.

* * *

More time elapses.

Maybe it is the next night—it might even be the next week, but sometime after he weeps, Horton discovers a voicemail from a man who claims to be a talent scout for a large agency in Los Angeles called Korngold, LLC, or something. Horton is surprised that his phone still functions.

In the voicemail, the scout explains that he has been trying for months to find the man from Banana Pancakes. Many people in the industry believe Horton shows lots of promise. He says that after spending days dissecting the thousands of pages of comments on the video, he noticed that the very first comments came from high school students, boasting that Banana Pancakes was their substitute teacher.

Very worthless comments, like:

It's Mr. Hagardy! Wow! A little too much to drink? LOL!!!

Mr. Hagardy likes 'em FAT! HAHAHA!

The scout says that after scrolling through the thoughtlessness, he found out the district for which Horton once worked, and from there, was able to finagle his way into some contact information.

Suddenly, Horton is being offered contracts and the kind of fame with paychecks—the scout says he sees something in Horton. Real potential. Real "talent."

"Sir," says Horton, "that video was a mistake. No talent or rehearsal went into it. Truth be told, I don't remember it."

The scout of Korngold, LLC enjoys Horton's honesty, says it's cute, and explains that people these days are "very, *very* stupid."

Subsequently, "talent" scouts no longer seek talent or even intelligent, craft-mastering people, but quite the opposite.

"Flukes and morons," says the scout over a cup of expensive joe, his treat, "they are now the demographic in want. They generate the money. You, Banana Pancakes, generate the money."

Horton is not tickled by the idea of making money off of, essentially, being a fucking idiot. This is not how Horton pictured things to play out. For years he has worked at garnering acclaim from the depth and creativity of his mind, not from being a fluke or a moron. He reads books, he writes, he thinks critically and feels he has a lot more to offer the world than a barbarous YouTube snippet. He would like to forget that night altogether instead of putting himself in a position where he will have to exploit it for more. The state of his life, however, does not leave him much of a choice. He has had no income for months, no food, his socks have holes, and so he signs with Korngold, LLC's talent scout without any clue of what to expect. Within a month, the scout, now Horton's agent, arranges a book deal.

Naturally, Horton wonders what his book will be about—he has never done *anything!*

The agent explains how the book will be a memoir on the ways alcohol has ruined Horton. Nearly all of it will be a lie. There will be steamy love encounters, which will be both enhanced and derailed by alcohol. Of course, in *real* life, Horton has rarely experienced intercourse. Some funny made-up bloopers will serve as comedic ease in the book, and there will also be some anecdotes of knockdown, bare-knuckle, black-eye brawls, when in reality, Horton has never been in a fist fight.

The agent promises to help Horton every step of the way,

from inventing and embellishing the tales to tying them all into a worthwhile story arc that makes readers laugh at Horton but pity him at the same time—the "dynamic one-two punch of a memoir," describes the agent.

Before the first word of the book is written, the agent begins preliminary arrangements for book tours and lectures at colleges across the country, where Horton will speak on the dangers of binge drinking—something he has only suffered the consequences of once. The agent also schemes to have Horton speak at middle and high schools, where he will identify the potential harm of YouTube. Horton will declare YouTube as the "globalization of cyber-bullying," a phenomenon that must be addressed by parents and faculty before it spirals out of control and torments young, innocent lives the way it has tormented him, an average man who now suffers under the curse of Banana Pancakes.

CYBER-FAME IS NO ONE'S GAIN

This will be the slogan associated with Horton's lectures, nationwide. It will attract the Dr. Phil-types. People everywhere will buy into it, the agent is convinced, *just* enough to watch Horton speak, but probably not enough to heed Horton's omens and actually monitor what their children do with their phones and computers.

"Parents have no control of their children anymore. Your lectures will make no difference, but that won't matter, see," assures the agent. "By that time, we will already have what we set out for."

Horton asks his agent if there might be an opportunity down the road for him to lecture or write a book about something that will actually have an impact on people, or at least something that isn't a bunch of *lies,* but his agent, who is experienced in the field, says, "I wouldn't count on it."

The agent is, however, able to arrange for Horton's publisher to front a hefty advance on the book he is about to author. Horton doesn't know what to make of this abrupt fortune. He feels it may be too good to be true. After all, who is Horton Hagardy in this world, and why would anyone care enough to *pay* to find out?

"You're *not* Horton anymore," reminds the agent. "You're Banana Pancakes."

Horton feels like a prize chicken in the hands of a man who, with experience and ease, can choose to caress him or snap his neck like a pretzel.

He can't quite get comfortable with all of it—it's not the typical career path. He figured he would substitute teach, publish some poems, maybe a collection, get a job as a teacher or tutor, and eventually be an established poet who made his own schedule and didn't get ripped to shreds daily by kids and administrators and colleagues alike. That would have been a simple life that Horton could get used to, but that path had been derailed and contorted into something quite the contrary: substitute teach → fall short as a poet → feel like a failure in a failing society → binge drink → make ill-advised statements → be famous for statements → have no identity other than Man Who Made Ill-Advised Statements → have no choice but to accept and embrace consequent identity. Soon, Horton will have a hard time differentiating between his personas, between the lowly, introverted skeptic and the man with the invented past who is famous for his aggressive attempt to "devour and plunder" a woman's ass. It could come to pose quite a challenge, a silly, scary challenge to balance these characters, and remember which is real.

"Just leave it up to me, Horton. Fifty million people—*and counting*—love Banana Pancakes and they will pay to know the man behind it. You already did your job. On March 17 of this year, you did your job. That's all it takes. You'll just have to trust me the rest of the way."

Horton sort of smiles, but not really. He finds it difficult to believe that the very people who made him destitute will soon pay for his lies. He has always hoped people were a little wiser, a little deeper than that, but if they make him rich, he'll know they're not. He'll know his agent was right.

Emil DeAndreis is a twenty-seven-year-old substitute teacher and high school baseball coach in San Francisco.

CPSIA information can be obtained at www.ICGtesting.com
Printed in the USA
BVOW03s2123201213

339730BV00014B/280/P